SCALES

Scales

Melographed by **CÉSAR VALLEJO**

Edited and Translated by JOSEPH MULLIGAN

WESLEYAN

UNIVERSITY

PRESS

Middletown,

Connecticut

Wesleyan University Press
Middletown CT 06459
www.wesleyan.edu/wespress
© 2017 Joseph Mulligan

"The Gravest Moment of My Life," by Andrés
Echevarría, originally written in Spanish
especially for this volume, was translated by
Joseph Mulligan.

Library of Congress Cataloging-in-Publication Data
available upon request

5 4 3 2 1

CONTENTS

ACKNOWLEDGMENTS

The decision to complete this translation was the fruit of conversations I had with Gladys Flores Heredia, Stephan Hart, Andrés Echevarría, Kenji Matsumoto, Jesús Cabel, José Antonio Mazzotti, and Antonio Gonzáles Montes, during and after the Congreso Internacional Vallejo Siempre, held in Lima in October 2014. Their encouragement and insight into the importance of *Scales* within César Vallejo's oeuvre were strong motivations for this project. I am especially grateful to Andrés Echevarría for sharing his photographs of the ruins of Trujillo Central Jail, along with his essay that accompanies them in the appendix, and for helping set the Castilian version included here. I am in debt to Jorge Kishimoto for generously allowing me to reprint photos of Vallejo from his private collection and to Beatriz Sosa for helping me gather materials essential to this volume. Some of my translations in this volume were first published in *Selected Writings of César Vallejo* (Wesleyan University Press, 2015); my deep gratitude to Suzanna Tamminen and her team for their remarkable contribution to an intercontinental vision of César Vallejo.

1. César Vallejo, 1923. Courtesy of Jorge Kishimoto.

Scales comes out of César Vallejo's experimentalist phase, which is to say, between 1919 and 1923, thus making it contemporaneous with *Trilce*. The writing produced by the Peruvian during that period shattered many aesthetic notions prevailing in Latin America and Europe at the height of avant-garde literary production. Yet locating *this* Vallejo in relation to *that* avant-garde proves inherently problematic, because he went out of his way to oppose the notion of formulaic production, and the literary schools in question were formed around manifestos of aesthetic prescriptions.[1] So if the proposal of *Scales* operates within the sphere of *vanguardismo*, it must be recognized as a heterodox iconoclast of that modern religion, not as an orthodox evangelist, as one might assume.[2]

For half a century after its first edition, *Scales* was read as an opportunity to contextualize Vallejo's poetry, seen as indisputably superior to his narrative prose by the first critics to address it, such as Luis Monguió, Jorge Cornejo Polar, and André Coyné.[3] The subordination of his narrative prose to his poetry proved untenable once Eduardo Neale-Silva showed how *Scales* contributed to the shift from romantic to modernist fiction by reconceptualizing the narrative mode and the depiction of the human circumstance in time and space. Since the late 1980s, interest in *Scales* and in Vallejo's prose fiction in general has grown to a degree that can no longer be overlooked.[4]

This introduction traces vital events relevant to the period of *Scales* and relates them to the other compositions that Vallejo completed before and immediately after it. Light is then thrown on major motifs and aesthetic features that provide readers unaccustomed to Vallejo's unconventionality with a way to approach his writing from the early experimentalist phase. This, in turn, leads us to observe how *Scales* contributed to the paradigm shift in Latin American literature that brought prose fiction into the modernist period.

❖ The years preceding the publication of *Scales* were marked by several deeply felt personal losses for Vallejo, coupled with the creation of multiple major works within his oeuvre and Latin American literature in general. In 1914 César's brother Miguel died in Santiago de Chuco, a terrible blow for the budding twenty-two-year-old poet.[5] The following year, under his adviser Eleázar Boloña, he completed his bachelor's thesis at the Universidad de Trujillo, *Romanticism in Castilian Poetry*, published by Tipografía Olaya. Vallejo's sharp generational awareness can be felt in his thesis, specifically in relation to José de Espronceda and his idiosyncratic poem *El diablo mundo*. Through this study Vallejo learned that art must not only reflect but refract questions that drive the artist to create. The poet can no longer look to nature, read the landscape, and reflect it in a work of art. He now requires transformation—a recasting of raw-materials-as-absorbed.

From July to December 1917, during the days of Vallejo's kindred bohemia and the rise of Grupo Norte, Vallejo dated Zoila Rosa Cuadra, whom he nicknamed Mirtho, as an "allusion to Gérard de Nerval's famous poem 'Myrtho' in *Les Chimères* (1853), in which refers to the beloved as a 'divine enchanteresse.'"[6] The couple's passionate breakup gnawed at the embittered poet, and in *The Black Heralds*, *Trilce*, and *Scales* his memories of her are recorded with anguish and heartache. This, however, would soon be overshadowed by the grief to come only one year later, when César's mother, María de los Santos Mendoza, passed away in Santiago de Chuco on August 8, 1918. Vallejo (and his writing) would forever be haunted by his mother's death.[7] Appearing as a specter in *Trilce*, *Scales*, *Against Professional Secrets*, and *Human Poems*, the mother is one of the most recurring motifs of his oeuvre.

A few months after his mother's death, Vallejo started dating Otilia Villanueva, who was the sister-in-law of one of his colleagues at Colegio Barrós, where he was teaching. This was also when he was completing his first book of poetry. The sort of spiritual thaumaturgy that Vallejo admired in Espronceda materialized in *The Black Heralds*, published by Souza Ferreira and distributed on July 23, 1919. It won him renown, not only through the department of *La Libertad*, but also in Lima, where he moved not long after its publication. From this early poetry onward, as Andrés Echevarría has recently explained, Vallejo proved time and again that he would not be a poet who writes facing a landscape but rather one who writes from a landscape, within it, surrounded by it.[8] *The Black Heralds* is an early example of this and may help explain how he successfully produced an indigenous aesthetic without succumbing to an indigenist itinerary.

The following year one of Vallejo's friends and a writer he deeply admired, Abraham Valdelomar, died in November 1919. The importance of Valdelomar for Vallejo is perceptible, at just a glance, in the articles "Abraham Valdelomar Has Died" and "Peruvian Literature: The Latest Generation."[9] Valdelomar played an essential role in Grupo Norte's openness toward new formal conventions in literature without the adoption of a doctrinaire theory of aesthetics. He opened the Trujillanos up to the postromantic vantage point of symbolists like Isidore-Lucien Ducasse and Jules Laforgue. This especially resonated with Vallejo, who went on to reformulate that argument between 1926 and 1928 to refute European literary schools for attempting to mint a formula of artistic creation and their Latin American counterparts for importing that technique of production.[10]

With the deaths of his brother, mother, and now an early mentor, Vallejo saw his losses compound and the stress fractures of a profound crisis start to show at the surface of his life. Added to that, Otilia was looking for a formal commitment from him, as they had been together for more than a year. Despite his feelings for her, he was not willing to marry. As a result of her ties to Colegio Barrós, his refusal to plan for marriage garnered him the administration's disdain, which became so unbearable that he finally resigned from his position, and by the end of July 1920 they had broken up.

On August 1 of that year, Vallejo returned from Lima to Santiago de Chuco, where riots had broken out in the wake of elections that had taken place not long before then. A general store, owned by Carlos Santa María, was set on fire, a bystander was shot, and two police officers were killed. With seventeen others, Vallejo was indicted. He was sought by police for almost two months, before being arrested on November 6 and detained in Trujillo Central Jail, where he would await a ruling for the next 112 days in the demoralizing conditions of a provincial jail cell.

The question of Vallejo's role in the events of Santiago has long been debated by critics. One of the most thorough documentations of the event has been provided by Germán Patrón Candela. At the time of his indictment, Vallejo's local celebrity would've been enough to garner the slander of an envious yet powerful Santa María, even though the official records state that Vallejo was seen holding a gun and was heard inciting others to take part in the riot. The traditional view holds that Vallejo was innocent and therefore wrongly imprisoned, whereas recent attempts have been made, namely by Stephen Hart, to suggest that Vallejo was guilty to some degree.[11] His later socialist commitments and defense of the Spanish Republic would seem to support Hart's claim, by revealing Vallejo's guilt in the events of Santiago in 1920 as an early instance of his radicalism before it matured into political ideology. This, however, remains speculation, and the likelihood that a successful young *cholo* like Vallejo would be attacked with slander is more than plausible.

The debate over Vallejo's innocence and guilt, in our view, is secondary to the reality of his imprisonment, which is to say that whether he was justly or unjustly imprisoned is not as important as the fact that he suffered for two and half months in that cell. The conditions were terrible; the privation, devastating; and the experience for Vallejo would never fully be erased from his memory. The moving letters and articles that have been preserved and that we include in the appendix of this volume bear witness to the anguish of Vallejo's confinement, as do the photographs of the prison taken in October 2015 by Andrés Echevarría and reproduced here. From prison Vallejo wrote an open letter to Gastón Roger, editor of *La Prensa* in Lima, requesting support from intellectuals and public figures in a desperate attempt to clear his name. The robust national response is astounding.

Roger wrote and published an article presenting Vallejo's appeal, and this was followed by letters of appeal by the great literary and social critic Víctor Raúl Haya de La Torre and Cosme D'Arrigo, a student at the Universidad Nacional Mayor de San Marcos. Additionally, as Patrón explains, the poet Percy Gibson contacted Hon. Carlos Polar, president of the Superior Court of Justice of Arequipa, who, in turn, transmitted Gibson's request to other magistrates. In the name of the intellectuals of Arequipa, minister of justice Hon. Óscar Barrós issued an official telegram to the criminal court of Trujillo requesting Vallejo's release.[12]

Similar petitions were also signed and submitted to the Trujillo criminal court by university students of Trujillo and by a conglomerate of Trujillo journalists from *La Reforma*, *La Industria*, and *La Libertad*. On December 30, 1920, Juan Francisco Valega, president of the Student Federation of Peru, sent his petition for Vallejo's release by telegram to the president of the criminal court of Trujillo. In Puno the important group Orkopata published several appeals for Vallejo's release in *Boletín Titikaka*. On

December 10, 1920, *La Reforma* (Trujillo) printed a petition signed by the directors of Chiclayo newspapers *El Tiempo*, *El País*, *El Departamento*, *El Bien Agrícola*, and *La Abeja*.[13]

Horrifying as Vallejo's incarceration was, it didn't stop him from writing—in addition to appeals for support of his release—some of the most celebrated literature of the first half of the twentieth century. The first section of *Scales*, "Cuneiforms," and several poems of *Trilce* were composed in his cell of Trujillo Central Jail. In effect, Vallejo wrote "from and about the prison."[14] As we later explain in greater detail, the figure of the prisoner counts as a major motif of *Scales* and a central register in the Santiaguino's biography. Although Vallejo wouldn't be acquitted officially for another seven years, on February 26, 1921, he was released on bail, thanks to the assistance of his attorney, Carlos Godoy.

Not long after his release, Vallejo completed his second book of poems, *Trilce*, published in October 1922 by Talleres Tipográficos de la Penitenciaría in Lima. As often happens with groundbreaking artworks, *Trilce* was largely misunderstood by its first readers, although Antenor Orrego did write an insightful prologue to the first edition.[15] Now recognized as one of the most radical books of poetry to come out of the first half of the twentieth century, it is also Vallejo's most experimental work in any modality, principally because of the extreme linguistic and metrical torsion to which he subjected his formally trained verse. Amid slashed Alexandrines and dangling *romances*, the poet of *Trilce*, in a cannibalistic performance that appropriates its form by devouring the object of its critique (reminiscent, in an inorganic way, of Oswald de Andrade's *antropofagia*), reveals an ironic stance of the modern subject under the sign of alienation.

Almost immediately after *Trilce*, Vallejo published *Scales* in 1923 with the same press, in a run of two hundred copies. While we examine *Scales* later in greater detail, we should mention here that this first adventure into fiction would extend into his next two endeavors—*Savage Lore* and *Toward the Reign of the Sciris*—the first of which he wrote and published in Peru just before leaving for Paris, and the second of which he probably started aboard the *Oroya* steamship that carried him from South America to Europe, where he completed it in the mid-1920s and unsuccessfully tried to persuade minister of culture Luis Valcárcel to fund a French translation of it for publication in Paris.[16] Composed concurrently with

Savage Lore and Toward the Reign of the Sciris were Vallejo's first newspaper articles, written in Lima, then in Paris, and published in El Norte (Trujillo). Although his gravitation to journalism is often explained as an attempt to put food on the table during years marked by economic pain, it may also be understood as a public medium permeable to poetic experimentation.

It is not enough to situate Scales within Vallejo's biography; it must also be read in the context of Peruvian short fiction published between the beginning of the twentieth century and its appearance in 1923. Antonio González Montes, who was the first to recognize this critical demand, has pointed to Cuentos malévolos, by Clemente Palma (Barcelona, 1904); Dolorosa y desnuda realidad, by Ventura García Calderón (Paris, 1914); La justicia de Huayna Capac, by Augusto Aguirre Moreales (Valencia, 1918); El caballero carmelo, by Abraham Valdelomar (Lima, 1919); Cuentos, by Lastenia Larriva de Llona (Lima, 1919); Cuentos andinos, vida y costumbres indígenas, by Enrique López Albújar (Lima, 1920); and Los hijos del sol (cuentos incaicos), by Abraham Valdelomar (Lima, 1921).[17] Vallejo sets himself apart from his contemporaries, to an alarming degree, when he decides to enter fantasy fiction with streaks of deep psychical revelations that blur into mystery and ambiguity, a technique that leads the narrator into modernity.[18]

To advance an epithet that Vallejo would later coin in Against Professional Secrets, we may say that, in Scales, his writing performs an upward fall in the discursive space of narrative.[19] Of course, this alone is not what sets the book apart from the literary trends prevailing in 1923, but its linguistic originality is particular to Vallejo's writings. The language of Scales, in many senses, is also the language of Trilce and appears nowhere else in the author's oeuvre with such intensity. In the context of Latin American literature, Scales marks the transition from modernista narrative—with its appetite for the strange, fantastic, morbid, and psychological (think Edgar Poe, Maurice Maeterlinck, Oscar Wilde, Gabriele D'Annunzio, Fyodor Dostoevsky, Arthur Rimbaud)—to vanguardista narrative, freed of traditional norms, and here Vallejo enjoys the company of Macedonio Fernández, Oliverio Girondo, Vicente Huidobro, and Martín Adán.[20]

❖ Soon after the appearance of the first edition in 1923, there was confusion over the actual title of Escalas, owing to the fact that the original cover read "Escalas / melografiadas / por / César A. Vallejo" (Scales / melographed / by / César A. Vallejo), as can be seen in the reprint at the beginning of the present volume. Because adjectives usually follow the nouns they modify in Castilian, some early readers understood the title as "Escalas melografiadas" (Melographed Scales). However, on the cover "Escalas" was in larger font than the rest of the text, and the title page omitted the word "melografiadas," so consensus has been reached that the official title of the book is "Escalas" and not "Escalas melografiadas."

According to Ricardo González Vigil, by employing this title Vallejo wanted to leverage the double meaning of "escala," that is, "a ladder that could be used to escape over the prison walls; and the musical scale, here made of six notes or texts that reach for the seventh, followed by a section called 'Coro de vientos,' to reinforce the musical element." The title of the first section, "Cuneiforms," he continues, "suggests a type of writing in the shape of wedges or nails, like marks made on the prison walls, or nails that torture the prisoner, playing off the musical notes of the melography, the writing on staffs, since it visually resembles the wedges of cuneiform writing."[21] The title of the second section, "Coro de vientos," is rich in polysemy as well. A "coro" is both a "chorus" and a "choir," while "vientos" are "winds" but also "woodwind instruments." Here and throughout we have translated this section as "Wind Choir," with the hopes of evoking the musical element and also the sort of howling proper to the dark gothic and fantastic worlds that the book explores.

The two sections of Scales are seemingly disparate, repellant, incongruous. The harsh juxtaposition of "Cuneiforms" and "Wind Choir" responds to a "clearly defined intention on the part of Vallejo to initiate the reader into his narrative."[22] The incongruity is not in vain, and the "Walls" of Scales are a prime example, since the author easily could have preferred "Eastern Wall" over "East Wall," to achieve uniformity with "Western Wall" and "Northeastern Wall," but instead we see a sign of his affinity for the irregular. By structuring the book with deliberate unevenness, Vallejo pits the two sections against each other, creating the inner tensions that allow him to test the permeability of the narrative form. In its most radical expressions, "Antarctic Wall" and "East Wall," this quasi-postromantic crisis of form becomes outright rupture and signals the direction of modern narrative prose. At any given moment in Scales, the narrative can be hijacked by poetic intuition and the enigmatic laws by which it abides.

If we can approach Scales by revisiting the author's biography and evaluating formal qualities of the work, we can also find ways to understand it by looking at recurring aesthetic motifs. Three of these, in Vallejo's early writings and especially in *Scales*, are the mother, the prisoner, and the madman. To speak of the mother is to speak of the home. In Vallejo's early writings the mother always represents an origin. James Higgins has shown this in relation to poem III of *Trilce*, where Vallejo adopts the voice of a child who is "seized by two fears: the fear of leaving the house to go outside into a dark and threatening world; and the fear of being left alone in the house, which is equally dark and threatening."[23] Leaving home is dangerous, but being left home alone is dangerous too.

In turn, the condemned man of "Windowsill" of *Scales* is transported to a "home" of his childhood by a memory of breakfast, only to hear his mother tell him that one day he'll be alone and she'll be dead. She's not there to care for him, and he experiences the peril of their separation. In "Beyond Life and Death," on the other hand, the narrator's mother is already dead and his journey home to mourn her, delayed by her supposed resurrection, culminates in irony and alienation. So leaving home is dangerous, but returning home is too. As a metonym for home, the mother reveals herself as either dead or moribund and, in this way, gives rise to the narrator's own vulnerability.

An equally powerful and unmistakable motif of *Scales* is the prisoner condemned not only to a jail cell but also to living a paradoxical existence. This notion of imprisonment, as an experience and also a metaphor of existence, has been explored in a penetrating analysis by Rafael Gutiérrez Girardot. While the motif of the prisoner is present in every text of "Cuneiforms," as well as in "The Release" of "Wind Choir," the prose poem "Northwestern Wall" proves to be one of the most fruitful texts of *Scales* for the study of this figure. Here, the imprisoned narrator tells how his cell mate has killed a spider, which leads him to ponder crime, justice, and the moment at which one human becomes the judge of another. For Vallejo, according to Gutiérrez, fate is unknowable, and reality can only be experienced.

Within the context of the jail, the experience of incarceration provokes a statement that devalues the accusation that put him there. "Justice is not a human function," Vallejo states. It "cannot be carried out by men, not even before the eyes of men." The consequence of that idea, Gutiérrez explains, "transposes the jail experience to his conception of the world." Without knowledge of our fate, but only nothingness and justice that "cannot be carried out . . . even before the eyes of men," the narrator can only pose a rhetorical alternative: "No one is ever a criminal. Or we all are always criminals." Since crime, in and of itself, can no longer be determined, given that there is no longer any justice to determine what is and what is not a crime, paradoxically, we all are always criminals.[24]

A similar paradox arises in Vallejo's formulation of the madman, the final motif we will mention here. The most eloquent example of this transpires in "The Caynas," which takes place in a remote town where some of the narrator's relatives believe that they are monkeys. When the narrator goes to visit them and discovers that the contagion has consumed his entire family, he finds his father and tries to convince him that he's human, that they all are human, but his father pities his son, "Poor guy! He thinks he's human. He's lost his mind."[25] If "The Caynas" smacks of "The Imp of the Perverse" by Poe (at least formally), it may be due to the narrator's madness, although it may also be due to the fact that the condition of madness itself had been popularized by early twentieth-century narrators emerging from the gothic strain of the romantic tradition, and because Vallejo appears to have wanted to move through the space that this opened up.[26]

From the work of Manuel González Prada, Vallejo had learned that the "death of God" entailed the dismantlement of traditional philosophical systems, along with religious and bourgeois concepts of life, society, and progress. The death of God is the end of the "*causa sui*," as Gutiérrez explains, which "erases the first link in the chain of cause and effect. Vallejo pondered and radically suffered this universal and personal situation and described it with the example of Luis Urquizo's madness."[27] His description keeps in tension the possibility of psychopathy and fantasy, as is the case in not only "The Caynas" but also "The Only Child," "Beyond Life and Death," "The Release," and, as we said, "Mirtho." Without a firm philosophical or religious foundation, self-identity is shockingly ambiguous, and Vallejo's fiction, at its height, dramatizes the character's struggle to attain it. His depiction of madness as a struggle for identity first appeared in *Scales* but went on to become one of his great obsessions.[28]

❖ With *Scales* Vallejo contributed to the shift from a prevailing post-romantic, symbolist tendency in Latin America to the wave of *vanguardismo* that flooded Latin American prose fiction in the first half of the twentieth century, by dehumanizing the narrative, depicting human circumstance as constant flow, proposing a new notion of time, a revised treatment of space, and a heteroclite sense of form. The identification of these achievements comes thanks to the labor of Neale-Silva, whose masterful study of *Scales* has been recognized throughout the field (and especially emphasized by Ricardo González Vigil and Antonio Gonzáles Montes) as not only the first comprehensive investigation of the work but also one that remains relevant today due to the acuteness of the critic's perceptions.[29] Since the gains of Neale-Silva do not seem to have been fully appreciated among many readers, we wish to outline some of his key ideas.

Although a strong character prevails in such texts as "Wax," the narration of *Scales* by and large is dehumanized, and the protagonists are no longer representations of actual persons but instead represent a "spiritual complex ('Antarctic Wall'), a symbol ('East Wall'), or an atmosphere ('Western Wall')." This dehumanization is especially felt in "Cuneiforms," where each prose poem is the "living personification of a serious inquiry," when it doesn't extremely reduce the character symbolically until its humanity is barely perceptible, as is the case with Mr. Walter Wolcot, from "The Only Child," or, in a more emphatic way, the anonymous character of "Western Wall." In the latter, the man is represented only by his beard, and its location is suggested by a seemingly insignificant detail — the "third molding of lead."[30]

In *Scales* Vallejo breaks with the aesthetics of analogy and expresses human circumstance as a constant flow.[31] The recounted events of the stories deliberately lack precision, along with "the uniqueness of perspective, the coherence of plot, and the submission to the empirical data and logical laws (with Aristotelian and Cartesian logic) that we find in 'traditional' fiction."[32] This divergence from the Western philosophical and literary tradition leaves in its wake established forms and fixed processes, so that it can propose "a dispersion, a flow filled with antithesis, in which there is a fusion of the true and the false, the beautiful and ugly, good and evil, the real and imaginary, life and death."[33] In this way, if we can't tell where the border is between "innocence and guilt or reason and madness, then we are just as ignorant to what divides life from death or oneself from another. . . . The obsession with limits (and with all that they oppose and exclude) proves disturbing and confounding in its different forms."[34]

In Vallejo's narrative universe, this flow of human circumstance must be understood as a discontinuous, disjointed flow, since the conception of time is subjective—an aesthetic feature that strays from traditional trends.[35] Rather than narrating a succession of events in a continuous temporal line, Vallejo transports the narrative thread to multiple planes, splicing the temporal aspect of the narration, in such a way that what is omitted turns out to be as relevant as what is recounted. Acquainted with the works of Dostoevsky, in *Notes from Underground*, for example, Vallejo would have been exposed to the free association of ideas or "stream of consciousness" and "inner monologue" that some critics have observed in his writing.[36]

The narrative space of *Scales*, in turn, is no longer the landscape that invites contemplation or reflects the soul of a character who elicits the reader's empathy, as was so dear to the romantics. "Nature," instead, "becomes a problematic extension, ruled by laws that defy human capabilities. . . . There is a lack of exactitude, limits, and geographical authenticity."[37] Vallejo emphasizes distances, the vagueness of locations, disproportion in general, and the mystery of horizons. The characters depicted in his early fiction feel alien to the land over which they wander, without a clear notion of who they are or what it means to head in the direction they're traveling, and in the chiaroscuro of that uncertainty, anxiety consumes them.

In *Scales* the narrative form itself undergoes a radical revision. The short story is no longer conceived as literary genre, with the rigid framework generally associated with it, but instead acquires an open structure, permeable to poetic and expository passages. This is, perhaps, most visible in "Cuneiforms," where Vallejo's prose poems or vignettes—particularly "Antarctic Wall" and "East Wall"—are on the same "lyrical-narrative path as Charles Baudelaire in *Paris Spleen*: a route that Vallejo will follow with the prose poems that he went on to write in Paris, not to mention some texts from *Against Professional Secrets*."[38] "Western Wall," however, on account of its concision and brevity, prefigures the genre of flash fiction in the likes of Augusto Monterroso.[39]

The writing of *Scales* moves in many directions, often at the same time, a characteristic of Vallejo's experimentalist phase that seeks to exploit the permeability of textual modalities. In a way, what is so impressive about Vallejo's early prose, of which *Scales* is exemplary, is not necessarily what it achieves but what it proves to be possible. Such possibilities have directed Latin American fiction toward the second half of the twentieth century, beyond the literary one-upmanship of high modernism, into a post–avant-garde moment, when the mode of fiction entails formal experimentation with poetry, and the content of prose narrative tells the story of posing its own potentiality.

JOSEPH MULLIGAN
Durham, North Carolina

THIS EDITION

The first edition of *Escalas* was published in 1923 by Talleres Tipográficos de la Penitenciaría in Lima in a run of two hundred copies. Since then, numerous editions of varying quality have been published with lesser or greater variations to the text. Aside from the verification of the correct title of the book, the neologisms particular to Vallejo's experimental phase can easily be confused for typographical errors and must be addressed with the utmost care. An edition like ours, however, intent on reproducing those neologisms, does run the risk of reprinting possible typographical errors.

There's another version of the text that cannot go unmentioned. It was delivered to Claude Couffon by Alice Gascar, sister of Rolland Simon. In 1988 Couffon reported that he had received this copy, a first edition of *Scales* edited by hand (probably around 1930) by Vallejo himself. According to Couffon, Vallejo had dedicated a copy of *Scales* to his father, and this copy somehow found its way to Paris, following his father's death, as a memento. Couffon claims that Vallejo's friend, Romain Rolland, had been looking for ways to publish the Peruvian's work in French translation during the late 1920s and into the 1930s and that he was the likely receiver of the manuscript that had been edited heavily to ease the burden of translation into French.

Couffon thinks that Rolland Simon probably asked Vallejo for a copy of *Scales* so that he could translate it, which is signaled by the penciled notes that translate or elucidate in French certain constructions in "Antarctic Wall" and "Windowsill." He thinks that Vallejo must have lent Rolland Simon his only copy, in which he'd made edits to lay out a definitive version, but because he died before he could finish it, the version was never completed.[1] And upon further consideration, the plausibility is there; French translations of Vallejo did appear in the 1930s, such as scene one of *La piedra cansada* (*The Tired Stone*) in French translation by Louis Parrot, who published it in *Commune* a few months after Vallejo's death in 1938.[2] It's not hard to imagine that this publishing objective could have at least been in the works in the early 1930s, especially since the second edition of *Trilce* had just been published in Madrid in 1928.

But that doesn't mean that we know for sure what the intention of the handwritten changes was. We do know that they undermine the aesthetic the 1923 edition had achieved. At this juncture, the edits seem to be of greater importance for biographical context than they do as a literary artifact. We therefore omit the Couffon manuscript from the scope of this translation, though not without inviting curious readers to consult it for further research or supporting the creation of a redline translation elsewhere.[3]

As for the edition presented here, we base the Castilian text on two editions of *Escalas*, edited by Ricardo Silva-Santisteban and Cecilia Moreano and by Ricardo González Vigil. The translation, in turn, has aimed to render a version that captures the author's tone and the bravado of his prose-poetry project in a way that disconcerts the reader. In an attempt to provide greater context to *Scales* and to Vallejo's biography, particularly what is related to his Trujillo imprisonment, we have included an appendix of additional documents in translation.

The aim of the appendix is to extend readers access to documents related to the events of August 1920 in Santiago de Chuco, the publicity campaign that ensued in Peru, and literary works that the author composed in Trujillo Central Jail during his three-and-a-half-month incarceration. Long obscured by literary myths, much of Vallejo's biography and the social context of his literary production has been unearthed by a field of scholarship that arose a half century after the author's death.[4] With this appendix, and the volume as a whole, we have endeavored to continue this trend of demystifying Vallejo's life in the presentation of his work and research on it.

scales

2. Cover of first edition, 1923. Courtesy of Jorge Kishimoto.

Cuneiforms

Penumbra.

The only cell mate left now sits down to eat in front of the horizontal window of our dungeon, a barred little opening in the upper half of the cell door, where he takes refuge in the orange anguish of evening's full bloom.

I turn toward him.

"Shall we?"

"Let's. Please be served," he replies with a smile.

While looking at his bullish profile thrown against the folded bright red leaf of the open window, my gaze locks onto an almost aerial spider, seemingly made of smoke, emerging in absolute stillness on the wood, a half meter above the man's head. The westerly wind wafts an ocher glitter upon the tranquil weaver, as if to bring her into focus. She has undoubtedly felt the warm solar breeze, as she stretches out some of her limbs with drowsy lackadaisical languor, and then she starts taking fitful downward steps, until stopping flush with the man's beard so that, while he chews, it appears as if he were gobbling up the tiny beast.

And as he finally finishes eating, the animal flanks out in a sprint for the door hinges, just as the man swings the door shut. Something has happened. I go up and reopen the door, examine the hinges, and find the body of the poor wanderer, mashed and transformed into scattered filaments.

"You've killed a spider," I say to him with evident enthusiasm.

"Have I?" he asks with indifference. "All the better: this place is infested anyway."

And as if nothing had happened, he begins to pace the length of the cell, picking food from his teeth and spitting it out profusely.

Justice! This idea comes to mind.

I know that this man has just harmed an anonymous, yet existing and real being. And the spider, on the other hand, has inadvertently pushed the poor innocent man to the point of murder. Don't both, then, deserve to be judged for their actions? Or is such a means of justice foreign to the human spirit? When is man the judge of man?

He who's unaware of the temperature, the sufficiency with which he finishes one thing or begins another; who's unaware of the nuance by which what's white is white and the degree to which it's white; who is and will be unaware of the moment when we begin to live, the moment when we begin to die, when we cry, when we laugh, when sound limits with form the lips that say, I. . . . He won't figure out, nor can he, the degree of truth to which a fact qualified as criminal is criminal. He who's unaware of the instant when 1 stops being 1 and starts being 2, who even within mathematical exactitude lacks wisdom's unconquerable plenitude—how could he ever manage to establish the fundamental and criminal moment of any action, through the warp of fate's whims, within the great powered gears that move beings and things in front of things and beings?

Justice is not a human function. Nor can it be. Justice operates tacitly, deeper inside than all insides, in the courts and the prisoners. Justice—hear me out, men of all latitudes!—is served in subterranean harmony, on the flipside of the senses and in the cerebral swings of street fairs. Hone down your hearts! Justice passes beneath every surface, behind everyone's backs. Lend subtler an ear to its fatal drumroll, and you will hear its only vigrant[1] cymbal that, by the power of love, smashes in two—its cymbal as vague and uncertain as the traces of the crime itself or of what is generally called crime.

Only in this way is justice infallible: when it's not seen through the tinted enticements of the judges, when it's not written in the codes, when there's no longer a need for jails or guards.

Therefore, justice is not, cannot be, carried out by men, not even before the eyes of men.

No one is ever a criminal. Or we all are always criminals.

Desire magnetizes us.

She, at my side, in the bedchamber, charges and charges the mysterious circuit with volts by the thousand per second. There's an unimaginable drop that drips and pools and burns wherever I turn, trying to escape; a drop that's nowhere and trembles, sings, cries, wails through all five senses and my heart, and then finally flows like electrical current to the tips. . . .

I quickly sit up, leap toward the fallen woman, who kindly confided in me her warm welcome, and then . . . a warm drop that splashes on my skin, separates me from my sister, who stays back in the environs of the dream that I wake up from overwhelmed.

Gasping for breath, confused, bullish my temples, it pierces my heart with pain.

Two . . . Three . . . Fooooooouuuuur! . . . Only the angry guards' voices reach the dungeon's sepulchral gloom. The cathedral clock tolls two in the morning.

Why with my sister? Why with her, who now must surely be sleeping in a mild innocent calm? Why did it have to be her?

I roll over in bed. Strange perspectives resume their movements in the darkness, fuzzy specters. I hear the rain begin to fall.

Why with my sister? I think I'm running a fever. I'm suffering.

And now I hear my own breathing rise, fall, collide, and graze the pillow. Is it my breathing? Some cartilaginous breath of an invisible death appears to mix with mine, descending perhaps from a pulmonary system of Suns and then, with its sweaty self, permeating the first of the earth's pores. And that old-timer who suddenly stops yelling? What's he going to do? Oh how he turns toward a young Franciscan who rises from his imperial dawnward genuflection, as if facing a crumbling altar. The old man walks up to him and, with an angry expression, tears off the wide-cut sacred habit that the priest was wearing. . . . I turn my head. Ah, immense palpitating cone of darkness, at whose distant nebulous vortex, at whose final frontier, a nude woman in the living flesh glows! . . .

Oh woman! Let us love each other to the nth degree. Let us be scorched by every crucible. Let us be cleansed by all the storms. Let us unite in body and soul. Let us love each other absolutely, through every death.

Oh flesh of my flesh and bone of my bone! Do you recall those budding passions, those bandaged anxieties of our eight years? Remember that spring morning warmed by the sierra's spontaneous sun, when, having played so late the night before, we, in our shared bed sleeping late, awoke in each other's arms and, after realizing that we were alone, shared a nude kiss on our virgin lips. Remember that your flesh and mine were magnetized, our friction coarse and blind; and also remember that we were thenceforth still good and pure and that ours was the impalpable pureness of animals. . . .

Oneself the end of our departure; oneself the alvine² equator of our mischief, you in the front, I behind. We have loved each other—don't you recall?—when the minute had yet to become a lifetime. In the world we've come to see ourselves through lovers' eyes after the bleakness of an absence.

Oh, Lady Supreme! Wipe from your bona fide eyes the blinding dust kicked up on winding roads and switchback through your concrete climb. And rise higher even still! Be the complete woman, the entire chord! Oh flesh of my flesh and bone of my bone! . . . Oh my sister, my wife, my mother!

And I break down into tears until dawn.

"Good morning, Mr. Mayor . . ."

Wait. I can't figure out how to start this. Wait. Now.

Aim here, right where I'm touching the tip of my left hand's longest finger. Don't back down, don't be afraid. Just aim here. Now!

Vrrrooommm. . . .

Very well. A projectile now baths in the waters of the four pumps that have just combusted in my chest. The recoil burns. Thirst fatefully insaharates[3] my throat out of nowhere and eats away at my gut. . . .

Yet here I note that three lonely sounds in complete domination bombard two ports and their three-boned piers that, oh, are always just a hair shy of sinking. I perceive those tragic and thricey[4] sounds quite distinctively, almost one by one.

The first comes from an errant tear that drips through the duct of a crocodile at night.

The second sound is a bud; an eternal self-revelation, an unending announcement. It is a herald. It constantly circles an ovoe[5] waist tender as a hand made of eggshell. Thus it always appears and can't ever blow past the last wind. So 'tis ever beginning, the sound of all humanity.

And the final sound. The final one watches over with utter precision, loudspoken during the close-out of all chatty glassware.[6] In this final blow of harmony, thirst dissipates (one of threat's little windows slams shut), acquires a different value within the sensation, is what it was not, until it reaches the counter key.

And the projectile that in the blood of my stranded heart
used to sing
and make plumes
in vain has striven to put me to death.

"Well then?"

"This is the one I've got to sign twice, Mr. Scribe. Is it in duplicate?"

On this swelter of a night, one of my inmates tells me the story of his trial. He finishes the abstruse narration, stretches out on his soiled cot, and hums a *yaraví*.[7]

I now possess the truth of his conduct.

This man is a criminal. His mask of innocence transparent, the criminal has been arrested. Through the course of his prattle, my soul has followed him, step-by-step, through his unlawful act. Between us we've festered through days and nights of idleness, garnished with arrogant alcohol, chuckling dentures, aching guitar strings, razor blades on guard, drunken bouts of sweat and disgust. We've disputed with the defenseless companion who cries for her man to quit drinking, to work and earn some dough for the kids, so that God sees. . . . And then, with our dried-out guts thriving on booze, each dawn we'd take the brutal plunge into the street, slamming the door on the groaning offspring's own fat lips.

I've suffered with him the fleeting calls to dignity and regeneration; I've confronted both sides of the coin; I've doubted and even felt the crunching of the heel that insinuated a one-eighty. One morning this barfly, in great pain, thought about going on the straight and narrow, left to look for a job, then ran into an old friend and took a turn for the worse. In the end, he stole out of necessity. And now, given what his legal representative is saying, his sentence isn't far off.

This man is a thief.

But he's also a killer.

One night, during the most boisterous of benders, he strolls through bloody intersections of the ghetto, while at the same time, an old-timer who, then holding down an honest job, is on his way home from work. Walking up next to him, the drinker takes him by the arm, invites him in, gets him to share in his adventure, and the upright man accepts, though much to his regret.

Fording the earth ten elbows deep, they return after midnight through dark allies. The irreproachable man with alarming diphthongs brings the drinker to a halt; he takes him by the side, stands him up, and berates the shameless scum, "Come on! This is what you like. You don't have a choice anymore."

And suddenly a sentence bursts forth in flames and emerges from the darkness: "Hold it right there! ..."

An assault of anonymous knives. Botched, the target of the attack, the blade doesn't pierce the flesh of the drunkard but mistakenly and fatally punctures the good worker.

Therefore, this man is also a killer. But the courts, naturally, do not suspect, nor will they ever, the third hand of the thief.

Meanwhile, he keeps doing pushups on that suspicious cot of his, while humming his sad *yaraví.*

I'm pasty. While I comb my hair, in the mirror I note that the bags under my eyes have grown even blacker and bluer and that in the angular brass of my shaved face the hue has scathingly jaundiced.[8]

I'm old. I wipe my brow with the towel, and a horizontal stripe highlighted by abundant pleats is highlighted therein like a cue of an implacable funeral march.... I'm dead.

My cell mate has gotten up early and is making the dark tea that we customarily take in the morning, with the stale bread of a new hopeless sun.

We sit down afterward at the bare table, where the melancholic breakfast steams, within two teacups that have no saucers. And these cups afoot, white as ever and so clean, this bread still warm on the small rolled tablecloth from Damascus, all this domestic morning-time aroma reminds me of my family's house, my childhood in Santiago de Chuco, those breakfasts of eight to ten siblings from the oldest to youngest, like the reeds of an *antara*,[9] among them me, the last of all, glued to the side of the dining room table, with the flowing hair that one of my younger sisters has just endeavored to comb, in my left hand a whole piece of sweet roll — it had to be whole! — and with my right hand's rosy fingers, crouching down to hide the sugar granule by granule....

Ah! The little boy that took the sugar from his good mother, who, after finding our hideout, sat down to snuggle with us, putting in time-out the couple of fleabags up to no good.

"My poor little son. Some day he won't have anyone to hide the sugar from, when he's all grown up, and his mother has died."

And the first meal of the day was coming to an end, while mother's two blazing tears were soaking her Nazarene braids.

WESTERN WALL

That beard flush with the third molding of lead.

Wind Choir

Stagnant rockrose of July; wind belted around each of the great grain's one-armed petioles that gravitate inside it; dead lust upon omphaloid hillsides of the summertime sierra. Wait. This can't be. Let's sing again. Oh, how sweet a dream!

My horse trotted thataway. After being out of town for eleven years, that day I finally drew near to Santiago, where I was born. The poor irrational thing pushed on, and from all my being to my tired fingers that held onto the reins, through the attentive ears of the quadruped and returning though the trotting of the hooves that mimicked a stationary jig, in the mysterious score-keeping trial of the road and the unknown, I wept for my mother who, dead for two years now, would no longer be awaiting the return of her wandering, wayward son. The whole region, its mild climate, the color of harvest in the lime afternoon, and also a farmhouse around here that recognized my soul, stirred up in me a nostalgic filial ecstasy, and my lips grew almost completely chapped from suckling the eternal nipple, the ever-lactating nipple of my mother; yes, ever-lactating, even beyond death.

As a boy I had surely passed by there with her. Yes. For sure. But, no. It wasn't with me that she'd crossed those fields. Back then I was too young. It was with my father—how long ago must that have been! Ah ... It was also in July, with the Saint James festival not far off. Father and mother rode atop their mules; he in the lead. The royal path. Perhaps my father who had just dodged a crash with a wandering maguey:

"Señora ... Watch out! ..."

My poor mother didn't have enough time and was thrown from her saddle onto the stones of the path. They took her back to town on a stretcher. I cried a lot for my mother, and they didn't tell me what had happened to her. She recovered. On the eve of the festival, she was cheerful and smiling, no longer in bed, and everything was fine. I wasn't even crying for my mother anymore.

But now I was crying more, remembering her as she was sick, laid out, when she loved me more and showed me more affection and also gave me more sweetbread from underneath her cushions and from the nightstand drawer. Now I was crying more, drawing near to Santiago, where I'd only find her dead, buried beneath the ripe fragrant mustard plants of a poor cemetery.

My mother had passed away two years earlier. The news of her death first reached me in Lima, where I also learned that my father and siblings had set out on a trip to a faraway plantation owned by an uncle of ours, to ease the pain, as best one can, of such a terrible loss. The country estate was located in the most remote region on the mountain, on the far side of the Río Marañón. From Santiago I'd head that way, devouring unending trails of precipitous puna and unknown blistering jungles.

My animal suddenly started huffing. Fine dust kicked up in abundance with a gentle breeze, blinding me nearly. A pile of barley. And then, Santiago came into view, on its jagged plateau, with its dark brown rooftops facing the already horizontal sun. And still, toward the east, on the ledge of a Brazil-yellow promontory stood the pantheon carved right then by the 6:00 p.m. tincture; and I couldn't go any farther, as an atrocious sorrow had seized me.

I reached the town just as night did. I made the last turn, and as I entered the street that my house was on, I saw someone sitting alone on the bench in front of the door. He was alone. Very alone. So much so that, choking on my soul's mystical grief, I was frightened by him. It must've also been due to the almost inert peace with which, stuck by the penumbra's half strength, his silhouette was leaning against the whitewashed face of the wall. A particular bluster of nerves dried my tears. I moved on. From the bench jumped my older brother, Ángel, and he gave me a helpless hug. He'd come from the plantation on business only a few days earlier.

That night, after a frugal meal, we stayed up until dawn. I walked through the rooms, hallways, and patios of the house; even while making a visible effort to skirt that desire of mine to go through our dear ole house, Ángel also seemed to take pleasure in the torture of someone who ventures through the phantasmal domain of life's only past.

During his few days in Santiago, Ángel did not leave home, where, according to him, everything lay just as it was left after Mom's death. He also told me about the state of her health during the days preceding the fatal pain and what her agony was like. Oh, the brotherly embrace scratched at our guts and suctioned out new tears of frozen tenderness and mourning!

"Ah, this bread box, where I used to ask Mom for bread, with big crocodile tears!" And I opened a little door with plain dilapidated panels.

As in all rustic constructions of the Peruvian sierra, where each doorway is almost always accompanied by a bench, alongside the threshold I'd just crossed, there sat the same one from my boyhood, without a doubt, repaired and shined countless times. With the rickety door open, we each took a seat on the bench, and there we lit the sad-eyed lantern that we were carrying. Its firelight went in full gallop onto Ángel's face, which grew more tired from one moment to the next, while night ran its course and we pressed on the wound some more, until it almost seemed transparent. As I noticed his state, I hugged him and, with kisses, covered his severe bearded cheeks that once again got soaked in tears.

A flash in the sky, without any thunder, the kind that comes from far away, during the highland summer, emptied the guts of night. I kept wiping Ángel's eyelids. And neither he nor the lantern, nor the bench, nor anything else was there. I couldn't hear. I felt like I was in a tomb.

Then I could see again: my brother, the lantern, the bench. But I thought I saw in Ángel a complexion now refreshed, mild, and perhaps I was mistaken—let's say he looked as though he'd overcome his previous affliction and gauntness. Perhaps, I repeat, this was a visual error on my part, since such a change is inconceivable.

"I feel like I still see her," I continued weeping, "without the poor thing knowing what to do about that gift, she keeps scolding me, 'I caught you, you little liar; you pretend you're crying when you're secretly laughing!' And she kissed me more than all of you, since I was the youngest!"

After the vigil, Ángel again seemed broken up and, as before the flash of light, shockingly emaciated. I'd surely suffered a momentary loss of sight, brought on by the strike of the meteor's light, when I found in his physiognomy relief and freshness that, naturally, couldn't have been there.

The dawn had yet to crack the following day when I mounted up and left for the plantation, bidding farewell to Ángel, who'd stay a few days more for the matters that had motivated his arrival to Santiago.

With the first leg of the journey behind me, an inexplicable event took place. At an inn I was leaning back, resting on a bench, when from the hut an old woman suddenly stared at me with an alarmed expression.

"What happened to your face?" she asked out of pity. "Good God! It's covered in blood...."

I jumped up from the bench and, in the mirror, confirmed that my face was speckled with dried bloodstains. A giant shudder gripped me, and I wanted to run from myself. Blood? From where? I had touched my face to Ángel's, who was crying.... But ... No. No. Where was that blood from? One will understand the terror and shock that knotted my chest with a thousand thoughts. Nothing is comparable with that jolt of my heart. There are no words to express it now, nor will there ever be. And today, in the solitary room where I write, there's that aged blood and my face smeared with it and the old woman from the wayside inn and the journey and my brother who cries and whom I don't kiss and my dead mother and ...

... After tracing the lines on my face, I fled onto the balcony, panting in a cold sweat. So frightening and overwhelming is the memory of that scarlet mystery....

Oh, nightmarish night in that unforgettable shack, where the image of my mother, between struggles of strange endless threads that later snapped just from being seen, became the image of Ángel, who wept glowing rubies, for ever and never![10]

I kept to the road, and, finally, after a week on horseback through the high peaks, temperate mountain terrain, and crossing the Marañón, one morning I reached the outskirts of the plantation. The overcast space intermittently reverberated with claps of thunder and fleeting sun showers.

I dismounted alongside the post of the gate to the house near the driveway. Some dogs barked in the mild sad calm of the sooty mountain. After so long I now returned to that solitary mansion, buried deep in the ravines of the jungle!

Between the garrulous alarm of riled-up domesticated birds, a voice that called and corralled the mastiffs inside seemed to be strangely whiffed by the weary trembling soliped, who several times sneezed, perked his ears forward almost horizontally, and by bucking tried to get the reins out of my hands in an attempt to escape. The enormous door was locked. I knocked on it mechanically. Yet the voice kept trilling from inside the walls, and, as the gigantic doors opened with a frightening creak, that oral doorbell rose over all sixteen of my years and handed me Eternity, blade first. Both doors had swung open.

Meditate briefly on this incredible event that breaks the laws of life and death and surpasses all possibility; word of hope and faith between absurdity and infinity, undeniable nebulous disconnect of time and space that brings on tears of unknowable inharmonious harmonies!

My mother appeared and wrapped me in her arms!

"My son," she exclaimed in astonishment. "You're alive? You've come back to life? What's this I see before me, Lord Almighty?"

My mother! My mother in body and soul. Alive! And with so much life that today I think I felt in her presence two desolate hailstones of decrepitude suddenly emerge in my nostrils and then fall and weigh on my heart until making me hunch over in senility, as if, by dint of a fantastic trick of fate, my mother had just been born and I, on the other hand, had come from times so remote that I experienced a paternal feeling toward her. Yes. My mother was there. Dressed in unanimous black. Alive. No longer dead. Could it be? No. Impossible. There's no way. That woman wasn't my mother. She couldn't be. And what did she say when she saw me? She thought I was dead . . . ?

"Oh my son!" my mother said, bursting into tears, and she ran to pull me close to her breasts, in that frenzy and with those tears of joy that she would always use to protect me during my arrivals and departures.

I had turned to stone. I saw her wrap her lovely arms around my neck, kiss me avidly, as though she wanted to devour me, and weep her affection that will never again rain down in my guts. She then grabbed my impassive face between her hands, looked at me head on, asking question after question. A few seconds later, I started to cry too, but without changing my expression or attitude: my tears were pure water that poured from a statue's two pupils.

I finally focused all the diffused lights of my spirit. I took a few steps back and stood before — oh my God! — that maternity that my heart didn't want to receive, that it didn't know, that it feared; I made them appear before the mysterious holiest of whens, till then unbeknown to me, and I let out a double-edged mute scream in her presence, to the same beat of the hammer that approaches and then withdraws from the anvil, as of the child who lets out with his first groan when he's pulled from his mother's womb, indicating to her that he's going to live in the world and, at once, that he's giving her a sign by which they can recognize each other for centuries on end. And I groaned beside myself.

"Never! Never! My mother died long ago. This can't be. . . ."

She sat up, startled by my words, as if she doubted whether it was me. She pulled me in again between her arms, and we both continued to cry tears that no living being has ever cried or will ever cry again.

"Yes," I repeated to her. My mother already died. My brother Ángel knows this too."

And here the bloodstains she'd noticed on my face passed through my mind as signs of another world.

"But my dear son!" she whispered almost effortlessly. "Are you my dead son that I myself saw in the casket? Yes! It's you! I believe in God! Come to my arms! But, what? . . . Can't you see that I'm your mother? Look at me! Look at me! Touch me, my son! What, don't you think it's me?"

I beheld her again, touched her adorable salt-and-pepper head, but nothing. I didn't believe her one bit.

"Yes, I see you," I replied. "I'm touching you, but I don't believe it. Such impossibilities just can't happen."

And I laughed with all my might!

THE RELEASE

Yesterday I was at the Panopticon print shops to correct a set of page proofs.

The shop manager is a convict, a good guy, like all the criminals of the world. Young, smart, very polite, Solís, that's his name, he's whipped together excellent intelligence and told me his tale, revealed his complaints, unveiled his pain.

"Out of the five hundred prisoners here," he says, "only as many as a third deserve to be punished like this. The others don't; the others are as or more moral than the judges who sentenced them."

His eyes scope out[11] the trim of who knows what invisible bitter plate. Eternal injustice! One of the workers comes up to me. Tall, broad-shouldered, he walks up jubilantly.

"Good afternoon," he says. "How are you?" And he shakes my hand with lively effusion.

I don't recognize him, so I ask him his name.

"You don't remember me? I'm Lozano. We did time together in the Trujillo penitentiary. I was so glad to hear that the court acquitted you."

Just like that. I remember him. Poor guy. He was sentenced to nine years in prison for conspiring in a murder.

The thoughtful man walks away.

"What!" Solís inquires with surprise. "You were in prison too?"

"I was," I reply. "Indeed I was, my friend."

And I in turn explain the circumstances of my imprisonment in Trujillo, charged with frustrated arson, robbery, and sedition. . . .

"If you've done time in Trujillo," he says smilingly, "then you ought to have met Jesús Palomino, who's from that department. He drained away twelve years in this prison."

I remember.

"There you go," he adds. "That man was an innocent victim of the poor organization of the justice system." He falls silent for a few moments and, after looking me in the face with a piercing gaze, decisively breaks out, "Let me tell you a little bit about what happened to Palomino here."

The afternoon is gray and rainy. Metallic machinery and linotypes painfully hang clanging in the damp, dark air. I turn my eyes and in the distance notice the chubby face of a prisoner who smiles kindly among the black steel bits in movement. He's my worker, the one who's paginating my book. This bastard won't stop smiling. It's as though he's lost the true feeling of his misfortune or has become an idiot.

Solís coughs and, with a toilsome inflection, begins his tale: "Palomino was a good man. It turns out that he was swindled in a cynical, insulting way by a hardened criminal never convicted by the courts, since he was from an upper-class family. Verging on misery, as Palomino was, and as a result of a violent altercation between these two, the unforeseeable occurred: a gunshot, a dead body, the Panopticon. After being locked up in here, the poor man endured sinister nightmares. It was horrendous. Even those of us who used to watch him were forced to suffer his hellish contagion! It was awful! Death would've been better. Yes, indeed. Death would've been better! . . ."

The tranquil narrator wants to weep. He noticeably relives his past with clarity, since his eyes moisten and he has to pause in silence for a moment, so as not to show in his voice that he's started to sob in his soul.

"When I think about it," he adds, "I don't know how Palomino resisted so much. His was a torment beyond words. I don't know through which channels he was informed that someone was plotting to poison him inside the prison and had been doing so even prior to his incarceration. The family of the man he killed prosecuted him far beyond his misfortune. They weren't satisfied with his fifteen-year sentence or with the way it dragged his family into clamorous ruin: they carried their thirst for revenge even lower. And then they would hide behind the cellar doorjambs and between one spore and the next of the lichens that grow on incarcerated fingers, in search of the most secret passageways of the prison; and so they would move around here, with more freedom than before in the light of day for this unjust sentence, and they would flutter their infamous ambushy eyelashes in the air that the prisoner had no choice but to breathe. Being notified of that, Palomino, as you'll imagine, suffered a terrible shock; he knew it and could do nothing from then on to make it disappear. A man of good stature, like him, feared such a death, not for himself, of course, but for her and for them, the innocent offspring skewered with stigma and orphanhood. Hence, the minute-by-minute anxiety and fright in the everyday fight for his life. Ten years had passed like this when I saw him for the first time. That tormented man roused in the soul no longer pity and compassion, but religious and almost inexplicable beatific transformation. He didn't evoke pity. His heart was filled with something perhaps milder and calmer and nearly sweet. When I looked at him, I no longer felt compelled to unlock his shackles or dress the blackish-green wounds that were open at the end of all his ends. I wouldn't have done any of that. In the face of such a plea, such a superhuman attitude of dread, I always wanted to leave him as he was, to march out step-by-step, startled, with pauses, line-by-line, toward the fatal crossroads, toward death under oath, so much has time revealed. Back then Palomino no longer sought help. He only filled his heart with something vaguer and more ideal, more serene and sweeter; and it was pleasant, a merciful pleasure, to let him climb his hill, to let him walk through the hallways in the dark, entering and exiting the cold cells, in his horrendous game of shaky trapezes, agonizingly flying toward fate, with no fixed point for him to catch. With his fleecy red beard and eyes polar-algae green, tattered uniform, skittish, abashed, he always seemed to see everything. An obstinate gesture of disbelief bounced off his dreadful just man lips, his vermilion hair, his mended pants and even his handicapped fingers that sought, in the full extent of his prisoner chapel, a safe place to lean and rest, without ever being able to find one. How many times I saw him at death's door! During work one day, he came to the print shop. Silent, pensive, taciturn, Palomino was cleaning some black rubber belts in a corner of the shop, and from time to time he'd shoot a most watchful glance at his surroundings, making his eyeballs furtively roll, with the visionary air of a nocturnal bird that catches sight of dreadful ghosts. He suddenly jerked back. On repeated occasions I had caught one of his coworkers casting, from one landmark to the next, noticeable expressions and uttering strange words of subtle aversion, perhaps without a reason, on the other side of the shop. Since their intention couldn't have been pleasing to my friend, given the background story I've already mentioned, such behavior caused him to experience an awkward jolt and a sharp stinging sensation that frayed his every nerve. The gratuitous hater, in turn, was surprised when he noticed this and, serenity now lost, poured out a few drops from a glass carafe with rather meaningful clumsiness and alarm; the color and density of the liquid was almost completely enveloped and veiled by a winged spiral of smoke coming from over by the motors. I don't know how to describe where those long mysterious tears ending up falling, but the man who shed them continued rifling through his work tools, each time with more visible alarm until he couldn't possibly have been aware of what he was doing. Palomino observed him without moving, overwhelmed by thought, with his eyes fixed, hanging on that maneuver that caused in him intense expectation and distressing anxiety. Then the worker's hands proceeded to assemble a lead ingot between other bars resting on the workbench. Palomino took his eyes off him and, dumbfounded, absorbed, downcast, he superimposed circles on the wounded fantasy of suspicion, released affinities, discovered more knots, reharnessed fatal intentions and summited sinister staircases.... Another day a mysterious guest came in off the street. She went up to the typesetter and spoke to him at length: their words were indecipherable with all the noise of the shop. Palomino jumped up, stared at her carefully, studying her from head to toe, pale with fear.... 'Look, Palomino!' I consoled him. 'Just forget about it; there's no way.' And he, in every response, rested his forehead on his hands, stained from being shut in and abandoned, defeated, powerless. Only a few months after they brought me here, he was the closest, most loyal and righteous friend I had."

Solís becomes visibly emotional and so do I.

"Are you cold?" he asks with sudden tenderness.

For a while the large room has been filled with a dense fog that turns blue in strange veils around the hourglasses of red light. Through the high-reaching windows one can see that it's still raining. It really is quite cold.

Notes from a distant sol-fa ring out, as if from between compacted cotton balls saturated by swarfs of ice. It's the penitentiary band rehearsing the Peruvian national anthem. Those notes resound, and in my spirit they exert an unexpected suggestion, to the extent that I almost feel the very lyrics of the song, syllable after syllable, set in, nailed with gigantic spikes into each of the wayward sounds. The notes crisscross, iterate, stamp, squeal, reiterate, and destroy timid bevels.

"Ah, what torture that man endured!" the prisoner exclaims with rising pity. And he continues narrating between ongoing silences, during which he undoubtedly tries to ensnare terrible memories:

"His was an indestructible obsession to keep from falling, consolidated by God knows who. Many people said, 'Palomino is mad.' Mad! Is it possible for someone to be mad who, under normal circumstances, is concerned for his endangered existence? And is it possible for someone to be mad who, suffering the claws of hate, even with the very complicity of the justice system, takes steps to avoid that danger and to try to put an end to it with all his exacerbated might of a man who deems everything possible, based on his own painful experience? Mad? No! Too sane perhaps! With that formidable persuasion over such unquestionably possible consequences, who gave him such an idea? Although Palomino had often exposed the hidden grim wires that, according to him, could inwardly vibrate to the very threat of his existence, it was hard for me to clearly see that danger. 'Because you don't know those wicked men,' Palomino grumbled undaunted. After arguing with him all I could, I fell silent. 'They write to me at my house,' he said to me another day, 'and they make me see it all over again; while my release could come soon, they'd pay any sum to keep me from getting out. Yes. Today more than ever, danger is at my side, my friend. . . .' And his final words choked me with thrashing sobs. The truth is that, facing Palomino's constant despair, I ended up suffering, at times, and especially as of late, sudden and profound crises of concern for his life, admitting the possibility of some form of even the darkest treachery, and I even verified for myself, arguing with the rest of the inmates, thereby testing, with who knows what kind of unexpected grounds of decisive weight, the sensibility with which Palomino was reasoning. But that's not all. Occasions also arose when it wasn't doubt I was feeling but an indisputable certainty of the danger, and I myself left him and went to the meeting with new suspicions and vehement warnings of my own, about the horror of what could transpire, and this is exactly what he did when he was calmly standing in some visionary oblivion. I loved him very much, it's true; his situation was of great interest to me, always scared stiff from head to toe; and I tacitly helped him search for the carabids[12] of his nightmare. In the end, I actually investigated the concealed pockets and minor actions of countless inmates and officers at the establishment, in search of the hidden hair of his imminent tragedy. . . . All this is true. However, given what I've said, you'll also see that by taking so much interest in Palomino, I slowly became his torturer, one of his own executioners. 'You be careful!' I'd say to him with foreboding anguish. Palomino would jump in place and, trembling, turn in every direction, wanting to escape and not knowing where to go. And then we both felt terrible despair, fenced in by the invulnerable, implacable, absolute, eternal stone walls. Of course, Palomino barely ate. How could he be expected to? He barely drank too. He might not have breathed. In each morsel he saw latent deadly poison. In each drop of water, each atom of the atmosphere, his tenacious scrupulousness nuanced to the brink of hyperesthesia made the most trivial movements of other people seem related to foods. One morning, someone at his side was eating a roll. Palomino saw him lifting the piece of stale bread to his lips, and in an energetic expression of repulsion, he spat in his face repeatedly. 'You better always be careful!' I'd repeat more often each day. Two, three, four times a day this alarm would sound between us. I'd let it out, knowing that this way Palomino would take better care of himself and thereby stay further away from the danger. It seemed to me that when I hadn't recently reminded him of the fateful disquiet, he just might forget it and then—woe betide him! . . . Where was Palomino? . . . Thrust forward by my vigilante fraternity, in a snap I made my way to him and whispered in his ear these garbled words: 'You better be careful!' Thus I felt more at ease, since I could be sure that for the next few hours nothing would happen to my friend. One day I repeated this more times than I ever had before. Palomino heard me, and after the ensuing commotion, he surely was thanking me in his mind and heart. But, I must remind you once more: on this road I crossed the limits of love and goodness for Palomino, and I turned into his principal torturer—his personal henchman. I started realizing the double meaning of my behavior. 'But,' I said to myself in my conscience, 'be that as it may, an irrevocable command of my soul has invested in me the power to be his guardian, caretaker of his security, and I shall never turn back for anything.' My alarming voice would forever beat alongside his, on his angst-filled nights, as an alarm clock, as a shield, as a defense. Yes. I wouldn't turn back, not for anything. Once, late into the night, I awoke in a sweat, as a result of having felt a mysterious vibrant shock in the middle of a dream. Perhaps an open valve of strife was throwing a bucket of cold water on my chest. I woke up, possessed by immense joy, a winged joy, as though an exhausting weight had suddenly been lifted, or as if a gallows had jumped out of my neck, all busted up. It was a diaphanous, pure, blind joy, I don't know why, and in the darkness it stretched out and fluttered in my heart. I fully woke up, regained consciousness, and my joy reached its end: I'd dreamed that Palomino had been poisoned. By the following day, that dream had overwhelmed me, with increasing palpitations at the crossroads: Death— Life. In reality I felt utterly seized by him. Harsh winds of unnerving fever charged my wrists, temples, and chest. I must've looked sick, no doubt, since my temples and head were heavier than ever and my soul mourned its grave sorrows. In the evening, it fell to Palomino and me to work together at the press. As they do now, the black steel bits were clanging, smacking into one another as if in an argument, scraping against one another. Hell-bent on saving themselves, they were spinning madly and faster than ever. Throughout the entire morning and into the afternoon, that stubborn irreducible dream stayed with me. And, yet, for some reason, I didn't shy away from him. I felt him at my side, laughing and crying in turn, showing me, impulsively, one of his hands, the left one black, the other one white, extremely white, and both always coming together with strange isochronism, at an impeccable terrifying crossroads: Death— Life! Life—Death! Throughout the day (and here I also forget why) not once did the vigilant alert from before reach my lips. Not once. My prior dream seemed to seal my mouth shut to keep from spilling such a word, with its right whitening luminous hand of fleeting, limitless, blue luminosity. Suddenly, Palomino whispered in my ears with a contained explosion of pity and impotence: "I'm thirsty." Immediately, driven by my constant obliging fraternity with him, I filled a reddish clay pitcher and brought it for him to drink. He thanked me fondly, clutching the handle of the mug, and he quenched his thirst until he could drink no more.... And at twilight, when this life of prickly carefulness became more unbearable, when Palomino had drilled holes in his head, on the brink of a breakdown, when a febrile yellowness of an old bone–aged yellow placated his astronomically restless face, when even the doctor had declared that our martyr had nothing more than fatigue brought on by an upset stomach, when that excessively peccary uniform was torn to shreds in corrosive agony, even when Palomino had formed his tall ephemeral smile—oh harmony of the Heavens!—with the wrinkles on his forehead, which didn't manage to jump down to his cheeks or to the human sadness of his shoulders; and when, like today, it was raining and foggy in the unreachable open spaces, and a causeless, labored, surly omen worsened down here, at twilight, he approached me and said, with bloody splinters of voice, 'Solís . . . Solís! Now . . . Now they've killed me! . . .

Solís . . . ' When I saw his two hands holding his stomach, writhing in pain, I felt the blow strike me at the bottom of my heart, the feeling of a roaring fire devouring my innermost recesses. His complaints, barely articulated, as if they didn't want to be perceived by anyone else but me, were floating toward my inside, like upward-flaring tongues of a flame long contained between the two of us, in the shape of invisible tablets. So surely and with such lively certainty had we mutually awaited that outcome! Yet after feeling as if the asp had seeped into the veins of my own body, a sudden, mysterious satisfaction came over me. A mysterious satisfaction! Yes, indeed!"

At that moment, Solís made a face of enigmatic obfuscation mixed with such deaf intoxication in his gaze that it sent me wobbling in my chair, as during a furious stoning.

"And Palomino didn't wake up the following day," he mysteriously added afterward, hoarse, without provocation, bearing many tons. "So had he been poisoned? And perhaps with the water I gave him to drink? Or had that only been a nervous breakdown? I don't know. They only say that the next day, while I felt obliged to stay in bed during the early hours, due to the overbearing distress from the night before, one of his sons came to inform his father that his pardon had been handed down, but he was nowhere to be found. The administration had replied to him, 'Indeed. The pardon of your father, handed down, he's been released this morning.'"

The narrator had in this a poorly contained expression of torment that drove me to say to him, with thoughtful consternation, "No . . . No . . . Don't start crying!" And, making a subtle digression, Solís again asked me with tenderness as deep as before, "Are you cold?"

"And then?" I eagerly interrupt him.

"And then . . . nothing."

After that, Solís falls dead silent. Then, as an afterthought, full of love and bitterness at once, he adds, "But Palomino has always been a good man and my best friend, the most loyal, the kindest. I've loved him so much, taken such great interest in his situation, helped to examine his endangered future. I even ended up investigating the contents of the pockets and deeds of other people. Palomino hasn't come back here, doesn't even remember me. That ungrateful bastard! Can you imagine?"

Again come the sounds of the penitentiary band playing the Peruvian national anthem. Now they are no longer singing the scales. The entire band plays the chorus of the song in symphony. The notes of that anthem echo, and the prisoner still silent, sunken in deep deliberation, suddenly flicks his eyelids in a lively flutter and cries out with a stunned expression, "It's the anthem that they're playing! Do you hear it! It's the anthem. But of course! It seems to be making out a phrase: Weee-aaare-frrreee. . . ."

And as he hums these notes, he smiles and finally laughs with gleeful absurdity.

Then to the nearby fence he turns his astonished eyes that glow with burning tears. He jumps from his chair and, stretching out his arms, exclaims with jubilation that sends a shiver down to my spine, "Hi Palomino! . . ."

Someone approaches us through the silent, unmoving, locked gate.

Yes. I once knew a man who underwent quite an undergoing. There was so much to it that I let myself get carried away by what happened to someone who, in all honesty, deserved curiosity and roomy meditations, on account of the terribly odd air to his way of being. . . . The city had thought he was mad, or an idiot, or well on his way to becoming one. Frankly, I'd say that I never regarded him in those terms. That's wrong. I did think he was odd, sure, but only because he possessed a truly greatocean[13] talent and a poet's authentic sensitivity.

Once we even had lunch at a hotel. Another time we had dinner. Yet another day, we had breakfast. So, for a period of four or five straight months, he lived alone, in the absence of his relatives. Laid back, the sentiment of our table. Even the good pale plates and cups smiled with a smart sheen on their limp teeth. One hell of a chatterbox, Mr. Marcos Lorenz. I looked dapper. Not long after I'd warmed up to him and started to wonder where he was, he never showed up at the restaurant.

Mr. Lorenz was a bachelor without any children. For ten years he'd been the boyfriend of an aristocratic city girl. For ten years. Wipe that smirk off your face. He was. In fact, Mr. Lorenz loved his beloved for nearly a decade. He told me himself and he said that she knew it too, despite the fact that they'd never been together even once, and maybe she did, since Lorenz often expressed his affection to her in writing. That old brand-spanking newfound love, trembling day after day, from the very fret, from the very self-sustained B-flat, until it had echoed[14] through all the ears of the district, where no one would ignore such a Neoplatonic tale, which, from the first page to the last, he embellished with slight typographical and possibly grammatical variations. That old brand-spanking newfound love.

"As if she has any love for me!" Lorenz would repeat at the table, forming a ball from an episcopal bite of a delicious corncob of May, which was falling apart and lactating tenderness between the silver fork's four prongs. Because, to tell the truth, my excellent fellow didn't seem to be all that certain of how the woman of his heart felt about him. To such a degree that, at times, her tranquility in the face of his uncertainty and the longevity of such a stale relationship became godless and made me think that it didn't amount to more than a respectful display of inoffensive vanity, on the part of Mr. Lorenz, since he was barely a citizen of the more or less herbalist sort, and she, a divine annelid of honey, born to make the most parched mouths salivate among the Solomons of the land. Then though came a test to the contrary, one morning when Lorenz walked into the restaurant. What had come over him? What did his face say with such tortuous factions?

"A smudge on the canvas, my friend?"

"It's nothing," he bellowed back. "She just walked by with some goon I've already learned is her fiancé. . . ."

"What?" I adduced sarcastically. "What about you? And your ten years of love?"

Mr. Lorenz walked inside, ordering a ham and sardine antipasto. Once he'd been served, he replied happily.

"It looks better than the one yesterday," and, as if a tiny bug bite had been bandaged, he shouted, "Waiter! Whisky!"

However, I was learning that Lorenz, with the red card of craving, really did feel an all-quadrant passion for that woman. No doubt about it. That old brand-spanking newfound love of his!

One afternoon not too long thereafter, I read in one of the local papers, "Wedding Confirmed: Marriage of Mr. Walter Wolcot and Ms. Nérida del Mar Officially Confirmed."

Oh! Poor Mr. Lorenz! What frozen shoulders.[15] Decade-long freezes! That divine annelid of honey was going to subjunct her golden aqueous name[16] to the trust fund goon whom Lorenz had learned was, in fact, Nérida's husband-to-be.

Terrible sadness befell my friend, as was to be expected, when he found out about that wedding. Placid table talk reached its end; and the golden waters and frothy Bénédictine of yore now may only have been weeping, dammed in the pupils of this new José Matías, who, ever since then, has always seemed to be on the brink of breaking into tears. That marked the end of the good humor that took aim at the fraternal effusion of sun-painted luncheons and endless flowery dinners in a joyful sunflower garret: even when Lorenz's appetite for good meals grew, as a result of his seventh romantic fail, chinny Pierrot aimed now at his wounded soul, now that days and night were pounding him with blue-bottled dawns of memory and the presence of yellow moons of absence.[17]

Mr. Lorenz didn't say another word about Nérida. Lost in thought, quiet, only from time to late did he inwindow[18] the mealtime sullenness by sneezing some verse from Ecclesiastes, among the ashes of which his misfortune would winnow with the stale air of orphanhood. Facing what could've been called a tragic palimpsest of love, on more than one occasion I endeavored to excavate the secret of his thoughts, with the goal of seeing whether or not I could somehow bring him relief. I couldn't. Each time I resolved to inquire, I sensed he put up a sealed stone barricade, his chest convex, against each question or secret.

Two thousand one hundred sixty-two hours later.[19]

And one Sunday near noon the orchestra lets loose a towerful[20] wedding march among the pilasters of rotted provincial moldings, under the temple's illuminated domes, whose high altar glows adorned with white orange blossoms dripping with countryside and with dew.

Given the procession's pomp, it was clear that Nérida and Walter Wolcot were the ones receiving the Almighty's blessing in matrimony; and, at once, the fate of beloved Mr. Lorenz—the lugubrious splash of anointment oil and black gloves soaked—was clearly burying ten weightless sarcophagi, in whose engraved fields of onyx, decorated in the Etruscan style, green limbs of flowering forget-me-nots were carried away by maimed supplicant Pierides, groves of live murmuring grapes, under skies of pure Anacreontic aniline, winds caught disrobing autumn trees, and mountains of eternal ice. Inside the ten sarcophagi, ten dead clocks were ticking....

That's how it all played out, really. The wedding couple was Nérida and the man of the quadruple U: he, balding prematurely, a stuffy scar-faced sort of incorrigible barfly who sleeps until three in the afternoon; his large greenbottle[21] eyes boastful, with an expression of chronic pleasure smeared across his face, as though he were always celebrating something; his suit brand new and with an almost mortuary British fit. As for her . . . visibly pale.

And the other? . . . Oh, what a spectacle of impiety and heroism! Mr. Marcos Lorenz was there too. I found him to be alarmingly upset. He saw me, but pretended he hadn't. I said hello with a nod of my head, and he paid me no attention. Very close to the couple stood that rigid man, petrified in Dantean wretchedness.

Wrapped in the finest fur-lined jacket, Monsignor meowed the sacred Latin of the sacrament in a gravelly voice. Grains of mystic resin burned in the old silver censers hanging on golden chains. For a second time the orchestra turned the sun-key of the score, and the sweaty acolyte, as if in a dream, mumbled his ritual syllables from one chapter to the next.

The sad bride suddenly did something strange. At the exact moment when the tonsured groom asks if she'll take his hand, she raises her dark burning amber eyes, flooded with febrile moisture, and pierces the other man, Mr. Lorenz. Distracted as she is, she doesn't respond. Some people from the procession acknowledge the unexpected silence and, following the direction of Nérida's gaze, noticed that it had been laid upon poor José Matías. For the duration of a lightning bolt, Mr. Lorenz met that gaze, abruptly broke his tormenting rigidity, and in one fell swoop threw himself on Nérida, rolling past anyone who tried to get in his way and, with the incredible swiftness of a bird of prey, took her shocked face in his hands and gave her a furious kiss on her virgin mouth, which parted like a furrow.... Mr. Lorenz then fell to the ground with a thud.

A commotion of voices and sudden paralysis in all. With seemingly haughty indignation, people drew near the outstretched kisser, the iniquitous intruder, an ear to his chest, heard Death fatigued and sweaty sit down to rest in that man's already frozen heart. Poor Mr. Lorenz! Only in this way, and only in this fleeting kiss, struck and lit for all his life, in death did Lorenz manage to unite his flesh to the flesh of his beloved, who may not have ever loved him in this world.

The wedding was thwarted. A blindingly dense dust-up arose between spouses-to-be. And at that same instant, Nérida had suffered a severe nervous breakdown that grew worse by the second, until she died an hour after the sudden death of poor José Matías....

And today, as ten or so years have passed since those two souls abandoned the world, on this golden January morning, a fine beautiful boy has just stopped on the corner of Belén, a boy strangely handsome and melancholic.

A bus stops and many passengers get off. One of them, a large man with an obviously mundane air to him, drops his cane. The boy, so beautiful and so very melancholic, goes to pick up the blood-red gilt cane, and he gives it to the owner, who's none other than Mr. Walter Wolcot himself. This man looks into the boy's face and, without knowing why, suffers a sharp pain. He thinks. Stuttering he finally thanks him for the kind gesture and, with desperate vehemence that weeps mysterious unrest, he asks the boy, "What's your name?"

The child doesn't respond.

"Where do you live?"

The child doesn't respond.

"How old are you?"

The child doesn't respond.

"What about your parents? . . ."

The boy begins to cry. . . .

An exhausted black fly comes and tries to rest on Mr. Walter Wolcot's forehead, until he walks away from the boy. Once he's gotten far away, he shudders several times.

Luis Urquizo let out a snort and, while swallowing his last glimmers of laughter, avidly drank his beer. He then smashed the empty mug on the zinc bar and shouted, "That's nothing! Scores of times I've ridden atop my horse as she walked with her four black hoofs sticking straight up in the air. Oh, my haughty claybank dun! She's the most extraordinary pachyderm on the face of the earth. And from riding her, what's surprising, wondrous, and spine tingling too is the stone cold spectacle of true lines and movements drawn by that foal when she stands in impossible gravitation on the underside of a plane suspended in space. I can't bear to see her like that, without feeling flustered and fleeing her presence, scared stiff and convinced my throat had been slit. It's awful! She looks like a gigantic fly clinging to one of those exposed beams that prop up humble rooftops in countryside villages. What a wonder! How sublime! How irrational!

Luis Urquizo works himself up as he speaks, his shaven face nearly gushing blood, his eyes moistened. He stumbles to and fro; he guillotines syllables, welds and ignites adjectives; he plays the horseman, makes feints; he funnels the broadest suggestions of his voice into algid interjections, hoists up his arm, waves, laughs: he's pathetic, he's ridiculous: he's infected with madness and shows it.[22]

"I'm out of here," he said as he ran out, leaping through the tavern doorway, and rapidly disappeared.

"Poor guy," everyone exclaimed. "He's lost his mind."

In effect, Urquizo was unstable. There was no doubt about it. The course of his behavior afterward confirmed it. That man continued to see things backward, confusing everything for everything else, through the five foggy lenses of his sick senses. As is natural, the good people of Cayna, the town where he resided, turned him into a target of cruel curiosity and daily distraction for children young and old.

After years without a cure, Urquizo's dementia became mortally serious and reached the trickiest and most edifying diorama of a man who has a two-angled triangle, bites his elbow, laughs when it hurts, and sobs out of pleasure: Urquizo managed to wander beyond the eternal corners,

37

where the seven central dyes of the soul and of color, like harmony and plentitude, bleed into one another.

It was around that time that I came across him one afternoon. From the moment I laid eyes on him as our paths were about to cross, I felt an unusual sort of mercy for that man who was so wretched and, that aside, was also my cousin in some remote bloodline on my mother's side; and, as I tried to get out of his way, greeting him as he passed, I tripped in a pothole on the cobblestone street and bumped into the sick man's fore-arm with my own arm.

"Not on your life! What are you, crazy?" Urquizo protested in anger.

The deranged man's sarcastic exclamation made me laugh and later became the motivation for numerous musings in which the mystery of reason sprouted thorns and, between my temples, pooled in the closed tempestuous circle of a disastrous kind of logic. Why that form of induc-tion by which he attributed to me the loosening of screws and disman-tling of motors that existed only in him?

This last symptom, in effect, surpassed the limits of sensorial hallu-cinations. Without a doubt, it now was more important, since it repre-sented nothing less than a type of reasoning, a tying of profound ropes, a sign of awareness. Urquizo must have believed that he was in his right mind; he must have been completely certain of it, and that, from his perspective, since I was the one who'd bumped into him, I was the real madman. Urquizo crossed that plane of normal sanity that almost all de-ranged people reveal—a plane that, due to its disconcerting irony, dam-ages and ridicules the healthiest of kidneys, until it removes our every mental rein and whisks away all of life's landmarks. That's why the sick man's southpaw exclamation punctured my soul so deeply and continues to prick my heart.

Luis Urquizo belonged to a large family from that area. Due to his mis-fortune, he was well loved by his relatives, who provided him all sorts of care and endearing assistance.

One day I was informed of a terrible event. All of Urquizo's relatives who lived with him had gone mad too. And there was more to it. They all were victims of one common obsession, an identical, zoological, gro-tesque, pitiful idea, a ridiculous phenomenon: they all believed that they were monkeys and lived as if they were.

One night my mother invited me to go with her and verify the state of our mad relatives. In their house, however, we only found Urquizo's mother, who, at the time of our arrival, was amusing herself by peacefully thumbing through a folder of old papers, in the light of a lamp that hung in the center of the room. Given that town's isolation and underdevelopment—it didn't have any institutions of social welfare or even police—those poor folks, sick in the head as they were, would go outside whenever they pleased, and that's exactly what we saw: they would roam through the town at any hour of day or night, entering homes, always rousing laughter and pity in everyone who saw them.

No sooner had the mother of the deranged espied us, than she began to shriek, furrowing her brows by force and, ferociously, raised and lowered them over and over again. Then with a mechanical gesture she threw the sheet of paper she'd had in her hands, and, curling up on the chair with the childish swiftness of a schoolgirl who wears a serious face in front of her teacher, she tucked in her feet, bent her knees alongside her neck, and in that unnatural position, similar to that of frozen mummies, she waited for us to enter the house, glaring with her whitecapped,[23] mobile, unexpressive, savage, spiderwebbed[24] eyes, which shockingly were those of a *Mico* that night. My mother clung to my side, frightened and trembling, and I too felt overwhelmed with the bone-chilling sensation of terror. That crazy woman looked furious.

But she wasn't. In the harsh glow of the nearby lamp, we discerned that her lost face, under short hair that drooped over her eyes in disgusting clumps, was then starting to scrunch up and move over the miserable raggedy trunk, twisting in every direction, as if being called by invisible means or mysterious sounds produced by an iron gate in a park. As though she'd ignored us completely, the woman began to scratch herself and pick out the fleas from her belly, sides, and arms, grinding the fantastic parasites with her yellow teeth. Every so often she'd let out a sustained shriek, scanning her surroundings and checking the door, apparently without noticing us. After a few long frightful minutes, my mother motioned for us to head out, and so we left the house.

It had been twenty years since that lugubrious night, when, after living apart from my family for that whole stretch of time, due to my studies in Lima, I turned into Cayna one afternoon, a village that, on account of its solitariness and remoteness, sat like an island on the far side of the lonely mountains. An old town of humble farmers, separated from the great civilized centers of the country by immense and almost inaccessible cordilleras, it often lived long periods in oblivion entirely cut off from the rest of the cities in Peru.

I must call attention to the rather disturbing fact that I had not received any news from my family during the six-year span of my absence.

My house was situated near the entrance of the settlement. A cinnamon-scented westerly May wind, one of those sweet and contemplative westerlies from the Peruvian Oriente, was wrapping its arms around the village, which for some reason right then, in its outer solitude and abandon, reeked of misfortune, exuding a stench of pity. The filth of neglect and inexplicable destruction oozed from all directions. Not one sole passerby. And barely had I rounded the first corner when my nerves splintered then frayed, suddenly overcome by a feeling of ruin; and without realizing it, I was about to break down and cry.

The rusted reddish gate of the family's mansion was wide open. I got down from the saddle and, huffing with lacerated tenderness, daunted with portentous emotion, speaking to the slow sweaty animal, I stepped into the hall. Immediately, among the noise of hoofs, guttural screams arose inside, as if they'd come from ailing souls howling through their delirium and exhaustion.

Now, I will not be able to say exactly what kind of rocky chains were wrapping around my sides, temples, wrists, ankles, until drawing blood, sinking in ferocious teeth, when I perceived that domesticated pack of something or other. The anthropoid image of Urquizo's mother instantaneously appeared in my memory, at the same time as I was stricken by a presentiment so much more powerful than my own strength that I had nearly attained a dire certainty of what, shortly thereafter, I was to face with all my being in the darkness.

I called at the top of my longs, almost groaning.

Nothing. All the doors of the rooms, as well as the door to the street, remained wide open. I released the bit from my horse's mouth, ran from hall to hall, courtyard to courtyard, bedroom to bedroom, silence to silence, and new grunts finally brought me to a halt in front of the mortar stairs that rose to the highest granary on the property. I peered up. Mystery was made anew.

No sign of human life—not even one single domesticated animal. Strange hands must have rearranged, with a cleversed[25] drift of taste and all sense of order and comfort, the usual layout of the furniture along with the rest of the belongings and furnishings of the home.

Guided by a secret abstraction, I quickly ran up the stairway and, about to step through the small door onto the terrace, I too caught clear sight of her. Inexplicable chilling tribulation stopped me dead in my tracks; swift doubt befell me and, aided by day's final glimmers, I scoured the space inside.

Horrifyingly enraged, denaturalized to death, a feral haggard face flashed among the shadows of that cave. Having mustered up all my courage—since I'd expected it all, my God!—I took cover behind the doorframe and forced myself to recognize that terrifying mask.

It was the face of my father!

A monkey! Yes. The entire truncated verticality and easy acrobatic boldness; the entire set of nerves. The entire poor facial carnation and wave; the whole frame. And, even the fuzzy fur—oh, the most subtle wool with which the seamless membrane of exactly is woven, the sufficient mathematical thickness that time and universal logic place, remove, and replace between one and the next column of life in motion!

"Grrr . . . Grrr. . . ." he growled and trembled.

I can confirm that he didn't recognize me. He did shift about rather agilely, however, as if to reposition himself more comfortably in the cavern where he'd taken refuge, although I don't know when; and, seized by the perturbation proper to a caged gorilla facing onlookers who agitate him, he was jumping, grunting, scratching the walls and plasterwork of the empty granary, without taking his eyes off me for a second, ready to defend and also to attack.

"Father!" I broke out in a plea, too powerless and weak to throw myself in his arms.

My father then exhaled a grunted diabolical breath, dismantled his untamed appearance, and, in a split second, seemed to salvage the entire night of his mind. Docile, smooth, tender, sweet, transfigured, human, he proceeded to slide my way, as he must have approached my mother on the day they stretched out so far and humanly that they made the blood they'd use to fill my heart and make it beat to the rhythm of my temples and the soles of my feet.

Yet just when I thought that I'd brought him back to clarity, with the miraculous spell of a brotherly cry, he stopped a few steps short of me, as if reforming himself in the mystery of his unwell mind. From behind a beard the expression on his emaciated face became so gaunt and distant, and nonetheless so strong from within, that it set me on edge until I had to look away, enveloping me in a sensation of coldness and a sheer break with reality.

Despite that, I spoke to him again vehemently. He returned a strange smile.

"The star . . ." he stuttered with deaf fatigue, before shrieking once again.

With that anguish and terror, I broke out in a glacial sweat, exhaled a dreadful sigh, rounded the stairway aimlessly, and left the house.

Night had finished falling.

My father had gone mad! He and all my relatives thought that they were quadrumanes, just as Urquizo's family had! My home had become a madhouse. The contagion of my bloodline! Yes, the fatal influence!

Yet there was something else. Something more atrocious and devastating had occurred. The whip of destiny; the wrath of God. Not only had everyone gone mad in my house, but all throughout the town and surrounding areas too.

Once I'd left the house, I started walking without knowing where I was headed or why, suffering every now and again moral breakdowns and upheavals so profound that neither before nor after did a similar bout ram so severely against my right mind.

The streets resembled walled-in roads. Wherever a passerby stepped in front of me, the simulation of an anthropoid, the mimicking of a person, leaped to his skin. The regressive zoological obsession, whose first seed sprouted so many years prior in Luis Urquizo's acrobatic head, had propagated in each and every inhabitant of Cayna, without varying its nature in the least. All those poor devils were stricken with the same idea. They'd all been bitten at the same curve of the cerebrum.

I have no recollection of a night more tragic and brutal, at whose bottom of cut-up edges only the natural light of the stars shone, since nowhere did I discern a single artificial light. Even the fire—fundamental work and sign of humanity—had been banned from there! As if through dominions of a still unknown transitioning animal species, I sojourned through that lamentable chaos where I was unable, no matter how much

I wanted and tried, to come across anyone at all who'd escaped it. Apparently, all signs of civilization had vanished from there.

Shortly after my excursion, I must have returned to my house. I suddenly realized that I was standing in the front hall. Not one sound. Not one breath. I broke through the reigning compact darkness, crossed the wide courtyard, and came into the hall on the far side. What had become of my father and the rest of the family?

Some serenity touched my stricken soul. I had to look for my mother, against all odds and without wasting a second, and to see her and know that she was safe and sound and to caress her and hear her cry out of tenderness and joy when she sees me, and to rebuild, in her presence, the whole broken-down home. I had to look for my father again. Maybe only he, after all, would be sick. Maybe everyone else would enjoy the full exercise of their mental faculties.

Oh yes, my God! I had deceived myself, without a doubt, when I generalized so slightly. At the outset I'd noticed my nervousness and how ill-disposed my excitable fantasy had been to build terrifying castles in the air. And could I even be certain that my father really had dementia?

A breeze of hope cooled my inner recesses.

Shot forth with delight, in the dark I entered the first door I reached and, as I stepped inside, uncertain, I staggered forth and unconsciously removed from a pocket a box of matches and struck one.

I was looking around the room when I heard footsteps coming down the hallway. They seemed to be stumbling.

Blood disappeared from my body, but not so much as to force me to drop the candle I'd recently lit.

Just as I'd seen him that afternoon, my father stood in the doorway, followed by some sinister souls shrieking grotesquely. In one fell swoop they put out the light I was carrying, howling with fateful mystery, "Light! Light! . . . A star!"

I stood frozen and speechless.

In an ungodly manner, I gathered my strength to desperately shout, "Oh, father! Remember, I'm your son! You're not sick! You can't be sick! Enough with that growling from the wild! You're not a monkey! You're a human, father! We're all humans!"

And I lit another light.

A snort stabbed my heart from one side to the other. And my father whined with heartrending pity, full of infinite mercy.

"Poor thing! He thinks he's human. He's gone mad...."

Darkness fell again.

Rushed by fear, I withdrew from that tenebrous group, my head tottering.

"Poor thing!" everyone exclaimed, "He's lost his mind! ..."

❖ "So behold, the whack job!" added sadly the man who'd made such a strange narration.

Right about then, his nurse, in a uniform of yellow scrubs and indolence, approached him and motioned for him to follow, at the same time as he engaged us, saying good-bye out the side of his mouth, "A good afternoon to you. I'll take you to your cell. Good afternoon."

The mad narrator of that story vanished alongside his nurse, who led him among the leafy black poplars of the asylum, while the sea was bitterly weeping and two birds kept fighting on Thursday's panting shoulder....

A lunatic for candor, I take shelter under the firmament's indigo fingernail and under the nine remaining nails of my hands I add, wrap up, and pinch the fundamental digits, with one at the bottom, toward the highest awareness of right sides.

A lunatic for love, with what heartburn I love her.

I found her, blowing in the wind her lilac veil, saying to the tender gravel of their temples, "My little sisters, don't fall behind, don't fall behind. . . ." Her breasts buck, boasting through the city of mud, with the stridency of orders and threats. The fearless body—oh, did it ever!—broke right on the corner: I suffered in my every tip, facing such beautiful heroism, facing the imminent sight of aesthetic blood smoldering, facing the martyr death of that lively carnature's[26] eurhythmy, facing the possible failure of a lumbar that resists or of a rebellious nervation that quickly gets snared and submits to the other side. Behold the Spartan victory of that torsion! And all the wisdom, in hot medallion, sifted the foundry of that nerve gorge, through my soul's every astonished mouth. And then her thighs and her legs and her prisoner feet. And especially, her womb.

Yes. Her womb, bolder than her forehead; beating harder than her heart, her heart itself. Falconry of the hawked futures of aquiline eyelashes fluttering over the mystery's shadow. Who else but he! Worshipped breeder of eternity, tubulated[27] with all the currents recounted or yet-to-come of thought and of love. Womb carried on the vaginal arc of all happiness, and in the very intercolumniation of the two legs, life and death, night and day, being and not being. Oh womb of woman, where God has his only inscrutable hypogeum, his only worldly tent in which he stays warm when he descends, when he ascends to the land of pain, pleasure, and tears. God can be found only in woman's womb!

❖ This is what a young friend of mine was saying yesterday afternoon, while we were walked down Jirón de la Unión. I was splitting my sides in sharpened laughter. It's obvious. The poor guy is in love with so many elegant, distinguished, beautiful women who stroll down Lima's main drag between five and seven in the evening. Yesterday the sunset was burning summer hot. Sun, luxury, flirting, sensual charm in all directions. And my friend was flaring up romantically and passionately, a man possessed through and through. Yes. Transformed into a lunatic for love, as he called himself with a mixture of pride and strife. A lunatic for love.

I said good-bye to him and, now alone, said to myself, "A lunatic for love. Fine. But, what did he mean by 'lunatic for candor,' that ironic apostrophe that inaugurated his gibberish?"

The boy visited me last night.

"Hear me out," he said, sitting down next to me and lighting a cigarette. "Listen to what I'm about to tell you here and now, since it's far too extraordinary to remain hidden in me forever."

He looked at me with piercing melancholy and, after casting several fearful glances at the windows of the inn, continued covertly and utterly serious, "Do you know the woman I love?"

"No," I replied right away.

"Perfect. You don't know her. And yet you laughed at the way I described her this afternoon. That was nothing. Those phrases were merely truncated shoots of the giant enchanted X that is the existence of such a fleeting creature."

And preparing for the hunt the discharged brow of someone who was to capture two invisible scoundrels, his eyes popped out of their sockets at least a meter, he made his teeth and even his gums grind against his gums, and from the lobes of his desolate ears to the tip of his nose, he flogged himself with a purple lightning bolt; frenetically he stuck both hands into the hedgehoggish mop of his hair as if to pull it out and with the voice of a visionary that almost made me burst into laughter, he slowly said, "My lover is two."

"You're still not making sense. Your lover is two? What do you mean by that?"

My friend shook his head, downcast.

"Mirtho, my lover, she's two. You laugh. That's fine. But soon enough you'll see the truth of that statement." And then he added, "I first met Mirtho in Trujillo five months ago, among a troop of my dear bohemian pals. Mirtho suddenly was pumping fourteen tonic Septembers, a miraculous ribbon of spring virgin blood. Ever since then I've adored her. Up to there, all was common and rational. But, soon thereafter, the most beloved and intelligent of my friends told me out of the blue, 'Why are you so mean to Mirtho? Knowing how much she loves you, why do you always leave her to go chase another woman? Don't treat the poor girl like that.'

"Rather than allowing that accusation, as unexpected as it was unfounded, to provoke my protest and lead me to reiterate my fidelity to Mirtho, I took it, as you will understand, only as innocent and slight calembour[28] of friendship and nothing more, so I smiled, though to the shock of my friend, who, given his austere and moral purity in matters of love, grimaced in reproach, insisting that everything he'd said had been in utter seriousness. However, I'd never been with any woman other than Mirtho, from the moment I met her. No doubt about it. My friend's complaint truly lacked grounds, and if it hadn't come from such a fraternal spirit as he, it would've left me at peace without nettling my conscience. But the nearly paternal affection with which that unforgettable friend has always treated the events of my life conferred onto such a strange reproach a somewhat unsettling touch worthy of attention to prevent him from hurting me without knowing why. Additionally, due to my deep love for Mirtho, it pained me that he should have disrupted our happiness.

"From then on, that friend continued to repeat his same old accusation, each time more acrimonious. I, in turn, kept trying to prove through all possible means that I was loyal to Mirtho. Vane attempts. Nothing. The accusation marched on and made its claim with such stubbornness that I'd begun to believe its irrational author, when the rest of the bohemian humans, one by one, started to find in my behavior the exact same flaw.

"'We've all caught you in the act,' they outrageously reprimanded me, 'and with our own eyes. There's nothing you can say to the contrary. You can't deny the truth.'

"And, in effect, if I had asked everyone who knew me about the truth of this matter, they would've testified to my amorous relations with the second woman as unbeknown to me as she was unreal. And my jaw would've dropped still further facing that phosphene collective, for nothing else could've occurred in the minds of my accusers.

"But one circumstance caught my attention, namely, that Mirtho never said anything that led me to believe, even remotely, that she was aware of my supposed infidelity. Not one gesture, not one prickle of her soul, despite her vehement and jealous character. Was she the only person in the entire city who didn't know about my guilt and didn't even suspect it amid the rumors flying every which way? And all the more so, if, as was already the word on the street, I had the habit of unscrupulously going wherever I pleased with the other woman. For all these reasons, Mirtho's unawareness was gnawing at my heart on the other side of everyone else's accusation. I was sure that in a mysterious way and through an inextricable chain of events, her unawareness continued the litmus test and perhaps even the reason behind my indictment.

"Without any doubt in the least, Mirtho didn't know anything about the other woman. There was no question. In the final analysis, hers was an ill-fated innocence, since she, although I know not how, started to give everyone else's lashing remarks such life, warmth, and — come on! — a sense of intrigue that I couldn't help but feel like I was being dragged to the ledge of a ridiculous position of bewilderment and absurd atony.

"Then, having taken Mirtho to the theater, we were standing in the lobby during one of the intermissions, when my eyes fell upon one of my friends. He recognized me at once and motioned for me to meet him in the foyer. Only a friendship as close as that could've gotten me to leave Mirtho alone. I excused myself and went to see my friend.

"'Now, you won't deny it!' he exclaimed from afar. 'Right now, you're with the other woman. . . . And what a likeness to Mirtho she bears!'

"I told him that I wasn't, that he'd been mistaken. It was useless. I said good-bye and returned to Mirtho's side, without having paid too much importance to what I understood as a simple game among friends at most.

"Numerous times after that, when I was with her, I would suddenly get (not without strong bouts of shock and alarm that, it's true, were short-lived) the feeling that I was with another woman who was not in fact Mirtho. For example, there was one night when this crisis of doubt culminated in frozen desperation, after I'd perceived an extraordinary afterglow of serenity in the unraveling waves of her silence — an afterglow completely foreign to all the pauses of her voice and bellowed throughout my heart that night. But, I repeat, those alarms stopped, when I started thinking that they must've been the obsessive suggestion that other people were making about me.

"Given what this could illuminate in such a mess, strange as it may seem, I must admit that aside from the time when I was introduced to

Mirtho, I never did see her joined by a third person, and there's more: whenever she'd meet me, it was only ever the two of us.

"Things continued that way, a growing nightmare that was going to drive me insane, until one warm and diaphanous morning when I was sitting in café Marrón, having a drink with Mirtho. Seated at the bare white translucent rubber table, we were alone.

"'Hey,' I painfully whispered to her, like someone who blindly clutches to a ledge, while her floating hands, spasmodically purple, rose to place her hair across her invisible temples. 'Do you want to tell me something?'

"She smiled full of tenderness and perhaps certain frenzy.

"'Hey, my beloved Mirtho!' I repeated in a stutter.

"She interrupted me violently and pierced me with her eyes of a female in rut, arguing, 'What are you talking about? Mirtho? Are you crazy? Who do you think you are?' And then, without letting me get a word in edgewise, she continued, 'Who is this Mirtho? Aha! The one you're cheating on me with? The one you love? You love another woman whose name is Mirtho. Isn't that something! That's how you repay my love.' And she wept inconsolably."

❖ The adolescent reporter fell silent. And, in the diffused glow of the screen, I seemed to see on both sides of the agitated boy, two fleeting forms come to life, softly rise up above his lover boy head, then blur with the high window, withdraw, and unravel in a telescopic flutter of eyelashes.

That night we couldn't smoke. All the bodegas in Lima were closed. My friend, who led me through the taciturn mazes of the renowned yellow mansion on Calle Hoyos, where numerous smokers converge, said good-bye to me and, with soul and pituitaries porcelained,[29] he jumped the first streetcar he saw and fled through midnight.

I still felt somewhat buzzed from our last drinks. Oh, my bohemia of yore, bronzemongery[30] ever cornered by uneven scales, withdrawn into the shell of dry palates, the circle of my costly human freedom on two sidewalks of reality that lead to three temples of impossible! You must excuse this venting that still emits a bellicose odor of buckshot smelted into wrinkles.

As I was saying, once I was all alone I still felt drunk, aimlessly traipsing through Chinatown. So much was clearing up in my spirit. Then I realized what was happening to me. Unrest emerged in my left nipple. A carpenter's brace made of a strand of black shiny hair from the head of my long-lost girlfriend. The unrest itched, smarted, shot inside and through me in all directions. So I couldn't sleep. No way around it. I suffered the pain of my stunted joy, its glimmers now engraved on irremediable ironclad sadness were latent in my soul's deepest brackets, as if to tell me ironically that tomorrow, sure, you got it, another time, swell.

So I had a craving to smoke. I needed to calm my nerves. I walked toward Chale's bodega, which happened to be nearby.

With the caution warranted by such a situation, I reached the door, put my ear up to it, nothing. After waiting a moment, I got ready to leave, when I heard someone jump out of bed, scampering barefoot inside. I tried to catch a glimpse, to see if anyone was there. Through the keyhole I managed to discern Chale lighting the room, sitting noticeably disturbed in front of the oil lamp, its pathogenic greenness in a mossy halftone welded to El Chino's layer of face, harangued by visible ire. No one else was there.

Chale's impenetrable appearance made him seem to have just woken up, perhaps from a terrifying nightmare, and I considered my presence importune, deciding to leave, when the Asian man opened one of the desk drawers, captained by some inexorable voice of authority. With a decisive hand he removed a laconic coffer of polished cedar, opened it, and fondled a couple of white objects with his disgusting fingernails. He put them on the edge of the desk. They were two pieces of marble.

Curiosity got the better of me. Two pieces—were they really marble? They were. I don't know why those pieces, at the outset and without my having touched them or clearly seen them up close, traveled though the space and barraged my fingertips, instilling in me the most certain sensation of marble.

El Chino picked them up again, angling egregious, flitting observations so that they wouldn't unscrew certain presumptions about the motive of his watchfulness. He handled and examined them at length in the light. Two pieces of marble.

Then, with his elbows on the table and the pieces still in hand, between his teeth he let out one hell of a monosyllable that barely entered his beady eyes, where El Chino's soul welled up in tears with a mixture of ambition and impotence. Again he opened the box perhaps out of an old determination that he now relived for the hundredth time, taking out several steel pieces, and with these he began to work on his cabalist marble pieces.

Certain presumptions, I was saying, jumped out in front of me. Indeed. I had met Chale two years prior. The Mongol was a gambler. And as a gambler he was famous in Lima; a loser of millions when he was at the table, a winner of treasures when speaking with peers. So what was the meaning of that tormenting all-nighter, that furious episode of nocturnal artifice? And those two stone fragments? Why two and not one, three, or more? Eureka! Two dice! Two dice in the making.

El Chino was working, working from the very vertex of night. His face, in the meantime, also was working out an infinite succession of lines. There were moments when Chale went into a frenzy and tried to break those little objects that were to be rolled on a felt-covered table chasing each other, in search of a random or lucky win, with the sound of one person's two closed fists pounding hard against each other until they emitted sparks.

As for me, I had taken considerable interest in that scene, which I could hardly think of leaving. It seemed to be an old endeavor of patient heroic production. I sharpened my wits, wondering what this ill-destined man was after. To engrave a set of dice. Could that be it?

This much is affirmed about digital maneuvers and secret deviations or willed amendments in the game's shaker. Something similar, I said to myself, comes through this man for sure. And this, because of what he rolled in the end. But what intrigued me most, as one will understand, was the art of the medium and its preparation, which had seemed to demand Chale's complete commitment. This is the correlation that must be preestablished, between the kind of dice and the dynamic possibilities of the hands. Since, if this bilateral type of element was not entirely necessary, then why would El Chino fashion his own dice? Any material kicking around would've worked. But no.

There's no doubt that the dice are made of a specific material, under this weight, with that edgility,[31] hexagonned[32] on this or that untouchable cliff to be bidden farewell by fingertips and then to be shined with that other dimple or almost immaterial coarseness between each frame of the points or between a polyhedral angle and the white exergue on one of the four corresponding faces. Therefore, it's necessary to bear the flair of the random material so that—in this always improvised (and therefore triumphant) point—it is always obedient and docile to human vibrations of the hand that thinks and calculates even in the darkest and blindest of such avatars.

And if not, one simply had to observe the Asian man in his creative, tempestuous task, chisel in hand, picking away, scraping, removing, crumbling, opening up the conditions of harmony and jaggedness between unborn proportions of the die and the unknown powers of his fickle will. At times, he'd momentarily stop working to contemplate the marble, and his depraved face would smile syrup in the glowing light of the lamp. Later, with an easy deep breath, he'd tap it, swapping one tool for another, and give the monstrous dice a practice roll, tenaciously inspect the sides, and patiently ponder.

A few weeks after that night, there were people amid scruffy crowds and others with similar opinions, who spread stupefying unbelievable rumors about amazing events that had recently transpired in the great casinos of Lima. From one morning to the next, the fabulous legends would grow. One evening last winter, at the door to the Palais Concert, an exotic personage whose goatee seemed to be dripping,[33] was speaking to a group of gents, who lent him all their ears:

"Chale had something up his sleeve, when he gambled those 10,000 soles. I don't know what, but El Chino possesses a mysterious unverifiable ability to summon when he's at the table. This can't be denied. Remember," that man stressed with sinister gravity, "that the dice El Chino plays with never appear in anyone else's hands. I'm talking about unmistakable facts drawn from my own observations. Those dice have something to them. What it is, I don't know."

One night I was driven by my distress into the hole in the wall where Chale used to gamble. It was an affair for the most ostentatious of duelers at the table, and many people were standing around the table. The crowd's attention, haltered by the ganglionic cloth covered with piles of money, told me that a low pressure system had set in that night. A few acquaintances led me through and encouraged me to place a bet.

There was Chale, at the head of the table, presiding over the session in his impassive, torturous, almighty appearance, two vertical straps around his neck, from the stumpy parietal bones of a bare hide to the livid bars of his clavicles, his mouth deceitfully forged in two taut pieces of greed that would never open in laughter out of fear of being stripped bare naked, his heroic shirt rolled up to his elbows. The pulse of life beat in him over and over, searching for the doors of the hands to escape from such a miserable body. Nauseating lividness on his predatory cheekbones.

He seemed to have lost the faculty of speech. Signs. Barely articulated adverbs. Arrested interjections. Oh, how the bronchial wheezing of the walking and living dead sometimes burns in each of us!

I decided to observe El Chino's minutest psychological and mechanical ripples as discreetly and meticulously as I could.

The clock struck one in the morning.

Someone placed a bet of 1,000 soles in the hands of fate. The air popped like hot water pierced by the first bubble of the ebullition. And now if I wanted to describe the appearance of the surrounding faces in those seconds of scanning, I'd say that they all oozed out of themselves, scrubbed and squeezed along with Chale's set of dice, lighting on fire and standing there in a line, until they needed and wanted to extract a miraculous ninth face on each die, as if it were the weary grin of Fate herself. Chale violently rolled the dice, like a pair of sparking embers, and he groaned a terrific hyenic obscenity that made its way across the room like dead flesh.

I touched my body as though I'd been looking for myself, and I realized that I was there, shaking in awe. What had El Chino felt? Why did he roll the dice like that, as if they had been burning or cutting his hands? Had the spirit of all those gamblers—naturally always against him—managed to do him harm, before a bet as lofty as this?

While the dice were released upon the emerald cloth, through my mind flashed the two pieces of marble I saw Chale engraving on that now distant night. These dice I saw before me certainly came from the nascent gems of yore, for I noticed they were of a whitened and translucent marble on the edges and of a firm almost metallic glow in the center. Beautiful cubes of God!

After a brief hesitation, El Chino picked up the dice again and continued to play, not without a certain convalescing spasm in his temples, which may have been perceived only by me. He threw them again, shuffled, threw them a second time, a third, fourth, fifth, sixth, seventh, eighth time. . . . The ninth landed: a five and a six.

Everyone seemed to dangle from a pillory and come back to life. Everyone became human again. Someone asked for a cigarette. Other people coughed. Chale paid 2,500 soles. I let out a sigh, swallowed my spit; the heat was stifling.

New bets were being made, and the tragic dispute of luck verses luck carried on.

I noticed the loss Chale just suffered didn't completely disturb him, a circumstance that cast an even greater shadow of mystery on the motive behind his previous unusual rapture of anger that, in view of the foregoing, couldn't be attributed to any bright nervous flash, since it was groundless and undermined my spirit's growing deliberations over El Chino's possible knowledge with currents or powers beyond concrete facts and perceivable reality. Just how far, in effect, could Chale get fate to side with him by using some infallible wise technique when he was rolling the dice?

In the first game that followed that other one with the 2,500 sol bet, the stakes were the same. Many other people joined in with bets lower than 500. And the combative ambiance around the banker waxed utterly hostile.

The dice jumped out of El Chino's right hand, together, at once, donned with the same thrust forward. With a measuring instrument that could register the most infinitesimal rigorous human equations of action in unnamable numerals, the absolute mathematic simultaneity with which both marbles were released could've been affirmed. And I'd swear that, while sounding the headlong relation that arose between those two dice at the start of their flight, that which is most permanent, most alive, the strongest, most unchanging and eternal in my being converged—all the powers of the physical dimensions fused—and this I could feel in the truth of my spirit during the material departure of those two flights, at the same time, unanimously.

Chale had thrown the dice while squeezing his entire sculpture into an anatomical deviation so rare and singular that it clouded my already-influenced sensibility. One might say at that very moment, the gambler had sterilized his animal nature, subordinating it to a single thought and desire while taking his turn.

In effect, how can one describe such a movement of his boney sides, grinding against each other, over the blare of a silence standing in suspense between the two pebbles of the march, such a rhythm of the shoulder blades being transfigured, brooding under truncated wings that suddenly sprout out, before the blindness of all the gamblers who perceived none of this and who left me at such a spectacle that punished me square in the heart! . . . And that unmoving confluence of El Chino's right shoulder was waiting for his forehead to finish gaining the rest of its arc, which the intuition and mental calculation of forces, distances, obstacles, accelerants, and even the maximum intervention of a second human authority were unfolding, shaking, adjusting from the highest point of man's soothsaying will to the bordering hills of divine omnipotence. . . . And that pallid, wiry, neurotic wrist, as if casting a spell, was almost diaphanized by the light that seemed to carry and transmit the dice in vertigo, which were waiting for it in the basin of his hand, jumping around, hydrogenic, palpitating, warmed, soft, submissive, perhaps even transubstantiated in two pieces of wax that came to a halt only on the farthest point of the table, as was secretly required, smashing down on the two sides that pleased the gambler. . . . Chale's whole presence and the entire atmosphere of extraordinary, unavoidable sovereignty that arose in the room right then and there had sucked me in too, like an atom in the middle of a solar fire at noon.

The dice were flying or, rather, running and stumbling over each other, skating, isochronally leaping at times, with the stabbing buzz of the snares that, in a stone drumroll, played a march of the irreversible, despite even God himself, before the poor faces of that salon, more solemn and congregated than at church when the consecrated host is raised. . . .

Along a trembling grayish line each die hobbled as it rolled. One of these lines began to thicken, started to unfold in stains some whiter than others; it then painted two black dots, then five, four, two, three, and finally stopped on the five. The other marble — oh, the sides and the back, the man and the front of the gambler! — the other marble — oh, the simultaneous departure of the dice! — the other marble advanced three finger-lengths more than the first and, in a similar process of evolution toward the unsuspected goal, also showed five carbon dots on the table. A winner!

With the serenity of someone who reads an enigma that long ago was familiar, El Chino placed the 5,000 soles from the bet in his bag.

"This is madness!" someone shouted. "The highest stakes always go to Chale. He's unbeatable."

El Chino, I repeated for myself, undoubtedly dominates the dice that he himself manufactured, and, in addition to this, since he's the owner and master of the most indecipherable designs of fate, they obey him.

The most powerful gamblers seemed to grow angry and grumble at Chale in the wake of the last game. The entire room rippled in a spasm of spite, and the muzzled protest of that crowd, whipped by fate's invincible shadow incarnated in the fascinating figure of Chale, was on the brink of becoming a bloodbath. One single great misfortune can do more than millions of various minor triumphs, and it allures and binds them in its hurricaned guts, until finally anointing them with its incandescent funereal oil. All those men must've felt hurt by El Chino's most recent win, and, had it come to it, they might've stripped the winner of his life. Right about then, even I — nettled by remorse as I recall — even I furiously hated him.

He followed it up with a bet of 10,000 soles. We all trembled in antici-
pation, out of fear and infinite compassion, as if we were about to witness
some heroic feat. The tingling tragedy spread through everyone's skin.
Eyes whinnied nearly pouring out grief. Faces straightened violet with
uncertainty. Chale tossed his dice. And with this single crack of the whip,
two sixes stared up at him. A winner!

I felt someone brush by me and push me aside to get to the edge of the
table, nearly breaking my neck with brutal depravity, as if an irresistible
deadly force were driving the intruder to such behavior. Those who were
next to me partook in the same gaping as I.

And instead of grabbing the money he had won, El Chino made it into
an unwonted oblivion so that, moving like a spring, he could immediately
turn his face back to the new contender. Chale's expression changed.
Both men's eyes seemed to collide, like two beaks that feel each other out
hovering in the air.

The newcomer was a tall man with proportionate and even harmo-
nious breadth, a lofty air, a large cranium on the sturdy horseshoe of a
lower jawbone that reposed in a collected manner, constructed with ex-
cessive teeth for chewing whole heads and torsos, and the slant of his
cheekbones widening downward. Minimal eyes, very sunken, as if they
withdrew only to later attack colorless girls in unexpected onslaughts,
taking on the appearance of two empty sockets. A toasted complexion,
coarse hair, curved and untamable nose, tempestuous forehead. The kind
of guy who takes to fighting, to adventure, who's unpredictable, full of
suggestions as bewitching as boas. A disturbing mortifying man, despite
his goodish well-centered looks. His race? One couldn't tell. That fleeting
human presence just may have lacked any ethnicity at all.

He had undeniable traces of worldliness and even appeared to be an
irreproachable club member, with his appropriate and distinguished suit
and the curious ease of his expressions.

No sooner had this personage assumed a position alongside the
table, than all the gas poisoned with booze and greed we breathed in the
casino—even that of the last game of 10,000 soles, the largest all night—
thinned out and suddenly vanished. What hidden oxygen did that man
bring? Had we been able to see the air, it would've looked blue, serene,
and peacefully azure. I suddenly snapped back to normality and the light

of my awareness, between a cool breath with renewed blood and relief, I felt freed of something. There was a peaceful expression on all the faces. The dominion of Chale and all his spellbinding postures met their end.

However, something over there was being born, something that at first took the shape of curiosity, followed by surprise, and then tingling unrest. And that unrest came forth, without a doubt, from the presentation of the new patron. Yes. For he—I would've affirmed so much with my neck—brought an extraordinary proposal, a mysterious plan.

El Chino was disturbed. Once he noticed the stranger, he didn't look at him face-to-face again. Nothing could get him to. I'm sure that he was frightened by the stranger and that, in him more than in anyone else present, the repulsive deplorable effect that man awakened was far too great to keep hidden. Chale hated him, feared him. That's the word: he feared him. What's more, no one had ever seen this gentleman in the casino. Even Chale didn't know him. This was also the reason why his presence was explosive.

The club member's breathing suddenly grew labored, as if he was hyperventilating. He huffed hard, glared at El Chino, whose downcast expression seemed crushed by that gaze, mutilated, reduced to pitiful ashes, his entire moral character, all his self-confidence from before, all his belligerence triumphing over fate now next to nothing. Chale, woeful as a child caught in the act, shook the dice in his right hand's trembling cupped fingers, wanting to demolish them out of impotence.

The crowd slowly turned its eyes to the outsider, who had yet to utter a word. Silence befell the room.

"How much are your winnings?" the newcomer finally addressed El Chino.

El Chino blinked, making an apocalyptical and ridiculous face of neglect, as if he were about to receive a deadly shot to the face. And turning in to himself, he babbled, without knowing what he was saying.

"That's everything."

The winnings were nearly 50,000 soles.

Mr. X named that sum, removed from his billfold the same amount of money and masterfully placed his bet on the table, to the astonishment of the onlookers. El Chino bit his lips and, still dodging the gaze of his new adversary, began to shake the marble cubes, his cubes. No one else joined in such a monstrously daring bet.

The solitary gambler, absolutely unknown to anyone except for El Chino, removed a revolver from his pocket, stealthily held it against Chale's head, with his finger on the trigger and the barrel aimed at its target. No one, I repeat, no one perceived this Sword of Damocles that remained suspended over El Chino's life. Quite the contrary, everyone saw it dangling over the stranger's fortune, since his loss had been taken for granted. I remembered what, just minutes before, had been whispered through the room: "The highest stakes always go to Chale. He's unbeatable."

Was it his good luck? Was it his wisdom? I don't know. But I was the first to foresee El Chino's victory.

He tossed the dice. Oh, the gambler's sides and back, his shoulders and his chest! With optimal eloquence, before my eyes the extraordinary spectacle repeated, the anatomical curvature, the polarization of all the will that tames and subdues, enters and performs the most inextricable plans of fatality. Again, before the creative force of the dice thrower, I was overtaken by a mysterious cataclysm that ruptured all harmony and reason for being of the events, laws, and enigmas in my stupefied brain. Again, that simultaneous release of the dice before the same fortuitous terms of the bet. Again, I opened my eyes, gorging them to verify the luck that was going to grace the great banker.

The dice tumbled and tumbled and tumbled.

The barrel and the trigger and the finger all waited. The stranger didn't look at the dice, he only stared terribly, implacably, at the head of El Chino.

Facing the unnoticed defiance of that revolver against that pair of dice about to paint the number that would submit to the invincible shadow of Fate, incarnated in the figure of Chale, anyone would've said I was there. But no. I wasn't there.

The dice came to a halt. Death and Fate had everyone at wit's end.

Snake eyes!

El Chino began to cry like a child.

Escalas

Cuneiformes

Penumbra.

El único compañero de prisión que me queda ya ahora, se sienta a yantar ante el hueco de la ventana lateral de nuestro calabozo, donde, lo mismo que en la ventanilla enrejada que hay en la mitad superior de la puerta de entrada, se refugia y florece la angustia anaranjada de la tarde.

Me vuelvo hacia él:

—¿Ya?

—Ya. Está usted servido—me responde sonriente.

Al mirarle el perfil de toro, destacado sobre la plegada hoja lacre de la ventana abierta, tropieza mi mirada con una araña casi aérea, como trabajada en humazo, que yace en absoluta inmovilidad sobre la madera, a medio metro de altura del testuz del hombre. El poniente lanza un largo destello bajo sobre la tranquila tejedora, como enfocándola. Ella ha sentido, sin duda, el tibio aliento solar, estira alguna de sus extremidades con dormida perezosa lentitud, y, luego, rompe a caminar a intermitentes pasos hacia abajo, hasta detenerse al nivel de la barba del individuo, de modo tal, que, mientras éste mastica, parece que se traga la bestezuela.

Por fin termina de yantar, y, al propio tiempo, el animal flanquea corriendo hacia los goznes del mismo brazo de puerta, en el preciso momento en que ésta es entornada de golpe por el preso.

Algo ha ocurrido. Me acerco, vuelvo a abrir la puerta, examino en todo el largo de las bisagras y doy con el cuerpo de la pobre vagabunda, trizado y convertido en dispersos filamentos.

—Ha matado usted una araña—le digo con aparente entusiasmo al hechor.

—¿Sí?—me pregunta con indiferencia. Está muy bien: hay aquí un jardín zoológico terrible.

Y se pone a pasear, como si nada a lo largo de la celda extrayéndose de entre los dientes, residuos de comida que escupe en abundancia. ¡La justicia! Vuelve esta idea a mi mente. Yo sé que este hombre acaba de victimar a un ser anónimo pero real y viviente.

¿No merece pues, ser juzgado por este hecho?

¿O no es del humano espíritu semejante resorte justicia?

¿Cuándo es entonces el hombre juez del hombre?

El hombre, que ignora a qué temperatura, con qué suficiencia acaba un algo y empieza otro algo; que ignora desde qué matiz el blanco ya es blanco y hasta dónde; que no sabe ni sabrá jamás qué hora comenzamos a vivir, qué hora empezamos a morir, cuándo lloramos, cuándo reímos, dónde el sonido limita con la forma en los labios que dicen yo . . . , no alcanzará, no puede alcanzar a saber hasta qué grado de verdad un hecho calificado de criminal es criminal. El hombre, que ignora a qué hora el 1 acaba de ser 1 y empieza a ser 2, que hasta dentro de la exactitud matemática carece de la inaccesible plenitud de la sabiduría ¿cómo podrá nunca alcanzar a fijar el carácter delincuente de un hecho, a través de una urdimbre de motivos de destino y dentro del engranaje de fuerzas que mueven seres y cosas en frente de cosas y seres?

La justicia no es función humana. No puede serlo. La justicia es inmanente. Ella opera tácitamente, fuera de los tribunales y de las prisiones. La justicia, ¡oídlo bien, hombre de todas las latitudes! se ejerce en subterránea armonía, al otro lado de los sentidos, de los columpios cerebrales y de toda convención humana. ¡Aguzad mejor el corazón!

La justicia pasa por debajo de toda superficie y detrás de todas las espaldas. Prestad más sutiles oídos y percibiréis su paso vigoroso y único que, a poderío del amor, se plasma en dos; su paso vago e incierto, como es incierto y vago el paso del delito mismo o de lo que se llama delito por los hombres.

La justicia sólo así es infalible: cuando no ve a través de los tintóreos espejuelos de los jueces; cuando no está escrita en los códigos; cuando no ha menester de cárceles ni guardias.

La justicia, pues, no se ejerce, no puede ejercerse por hombres, ni a los ojos de los hombres. Nadie es delincuente nunca. O todos somos delincuentes siempre.

El deseo nos imanta.

Ella, a mi lado, en la alcoba, carga y carga el circuito misterioso de mil en mil voltios por segundo. Hay una gota imponderable que corre y se encrespa y arde en todos mis vasos, pugnando por salir; que no está en ninguna parte y vibra, canta, llora y muge en mis cinco sentidos y en mi corazón; y que, por fin, afluye, como corriente eléctrica a las puntas. . . .

De pronto me incorporo, salto sobre la mujer tumbada, que me franquea dulcemente su calurosa acogida, y luego . . . una gota tibia que resbala por mi carne, me separa de mi hermana que se queda en el ambiente del sueño del cual despierto sobresaltado.

Sofocado, confundido, toriondas las sienes, agudamente el corazón me duele.

Dos . . . Tres . . . Cuaaaaaatroooooo! . . . Sólo las irritadas voces de los centinelas llegan hasta la tumbal oscuridad del calabozo. Poco después, el reloj de la catedral da las dos de la madrugada.

¿Por qué con mi hermana? ¿Por qué con ella, que a esta hora estará seguramente durmiendo en apacible e inocente sosiego? ¿Por qué, pues, precisamente con ella?

Me revuelvo en el lecho. Rebullen en la sombra perspectivas extrañas, borrosos fantasmas; oigo que empieza a llover.

¿Por qué con mi hermana? Creo que tengo fiebre. Sufro.

Ahora oigo mi propia respiración que choca, sube y baja rasguñando la almohada. ¿Es mi respiración? Un aliento cartilaginoso de invisible moribundo parece mezclarse a mi aliento, descolgándose acaso de un sistema pulmonar de Soles y trasegándose luego sudoroso en las primeras porosidades de la tierra . . . ¿Y aquel anciano que de súbito deja de clamar? ¿Qué va a hacer? ¡Ah! Dirígese hacia un franciscano joven que se yergue, hincadas las rodillas imperiales en el fondo de un crepúsculo, como a los pies de ruidoso altar mayor; va a él, y arranca con airado ademán el manteo de amplio corte cardenalicio que vestía el sacerdote. . . . Vuelvo la cara. ¡Ah inmenso palpitante cono de sombra, en cuyo lejano vértice nebuloso resplandece, último lindero, una mujer desnuda en carne viva! . . .

¡Oh mujer! Deja que nos amemos a toda totalidad. Deja que nos abrasemos en todos los crisoles. Deja que nos lavemos en todas las tempestades. Deja que nos unamos en alma y cuerpo. Deja que nos amemos absolutamente, a toda muerte.

¡Oh carne de mis carnes y hueso de mis huesos! ¿Te acuerdas de aquellos deseos en botón, de aquellas ansias vendadas de nuestros ocho años? Acuérdate de aquella mañana vernal, de sol y salvajez de sierra, cuando, habiendo jugado tanto la noche anterior, y quedándonos dormidos los dos en un mismo lecho, despertamos abrazados, y, luego de advertirnos a solas, nos dimos un beso desnudo en todo el cogollo de nuestros labios vírgenes; acuérdate que allí nuestras carnes atrajéronse, restregándose duramente y a ciegas; y acuérdate también que ambos seguimos después siendo buenos y puros con pureza intangible de animales....

Uno mismo el cabo de nuestra partida; uno mismo el ecuador albino de nuestra travesía, tú adelante, yo más tarde. Ambos nos hemos querido ¿no recuerdas? cuando aún el minuto no se había hecho vida para nosotros; ambos luego en el mundo hemos venido a reconocernos como dos amantes después de oscura ausencia.

¡Oh Soberana! Lava tus pupilas verdaderas del polvo de los recodos del camino que las cubre y, cegándolas, tergiversa tus sesgos sustanciales. ¡Y sube arriba, más arriba, todavía! ¡Sé toda la mujer, toda la cuerda! ¡Oh carne de mi carne y hueso de mis huesos!... ¡Oh hermana mía, esposa mía, madre mía!...

Y me suelto a llorar hasta el alba.

—Buenos días, señor alcalde...

Esperaos. No atino ahora cómo empezar. Esperaos. Ya.
Apuntad aquí, donde apoyo la yema del dedo más largo de mi zurda.
No retrocedáis, no tengáis miedo. Apuntad no más. ¡Ya!
Brrrum. . . .
Muy bien. Se baña ahora el proyectil en las aguas de las cuatro bombas que acaban de estallar dentro de mi pecho. El rebufo me quema. De pronto la sed aciagamente ensahara mi garganta y me devora las entrañas. . . .
Mas he aquí que tres sonidos solos bombardean a plena soberanía los dos puertos con muelles de tres huesecillos que están siempre en un pelo ¡ay! de naufragar. Percibo esos sonidos trágicos y treses, bien distintamente, casi uno por uno.
El primero viene desde una rota y errante hebra del vello que decrece en la lengua de la noche.
El segundo sonido es un botón; está siempre revelándose siempre en anunciación. Es un heraldo. Circula constantemente por una suave cadera de óvoe, como de la mano de una cascara de huevo. Tal siempre está asomado, y no parece trasponer el último viento nunca. Pues él está empezando en todo tiempo. Es un sonido de entera humanidad.
Y el último. El último vigila a toda precisión, altopado al remate de todos los vasos comunicantes. En este último golpe de armonía la sed desaparece (ciérrase una de las ventanillas del acecho), cambia de valor en la sensación, es lo que no era, hasta alcanzar la llave contraria.
Y el proyectil que en la sangre de mi corazón destrozado
cantaba
y hacía palmas,
en vano ha forcejeado por darme la muerte.
—¿Y bien?
—Con ésta son dos veces que firmo, señor escribano. ¿Es por duplicado?

Uno de mis compañeros de celda, en esta noche calurosa, me cuenta la leyenda de su causa. Termina la abstrusa narración, se tiende sobre su sórdida tarima y tararea un yaraví.

Yo poseo ya la verdad de su conducta.

Este hombre es delincuente. A través de su máscara de inocencia, el criminal hace denunciado. Durante su jerigonza, mi alma le ha seguido, paso a paso, en la maniobra prohibida. Hemos entrambos festinados días y noches de holgazanería, enjaezada de arrogantes alcoholes, dentaduras carcajeantes, cordajes dolientes de guitarra, navajas en guardia, crápulas hasta el sudor y el hastío. Hemos disputado con la inerme compañera, que llora para que ya no beba el marido y para que trabaje y gane los centavos para los pequeños, que para ellos Dios verá. . . . Y luego, con las entrañas resecas y ávidas de alcohol, dimos cada madrugada el salto brutal a la calle, cerrando la puerta sobre los belfos mismos de la prole gemebunda.

Yo he sufrido con él también los fugaces llamados a la dignidad y a la regeneración; he confrontado las dos caras de la medalla, he dudado y hasta he sentido crujir el talón que insinuaba la media vuelta. Alguna mañana tuvo pena el tabernario, pensó en ser formal y honrado, salió a buscar trabajo, luego tropezó con el amigo y de nuevo la bilis fue cortada. Al fin la necesidad le hizo robar. Y ahora, por lo que arroja ya su instrucción penal, no tardará la condena.

Este hombre es un ladrón.

Pero es también asesino.

Una de aquellas noches de más crepitante embriaguez, ambuló a solas por cruentas encrucijadas del arrabal, y he aquí que sálele al paso, de modo casual, un viejo camarada obrero que a la sazón toma honestamente de su labor, rumbo al descanso del hogar. Le toma por el brazo, le invita, le obliga a compartir de su aventura, a lo que el probo accede a su pesar.

Vadeando hasta diez codos de tierra, de madrugada vuelven a lo largo de negros callejones. El varón sin tacha le arresta al bebedor diptongos de alerta; le endereza por la cintura, le equilibra, le increpa sus heces ver- gonzante.

—¡Anda! Esto te gusta. Tú ya no tienes remedio.

Y de súbito estalla flamígera sentencia que emerge de la sombra:

—¡Aguántate!

Un asalto de anónimos cuchillos. Y errado el blanco del ataque, no va la hoja a rajar la carne del borracho, y al buen trabajador le toca por equí- voco la puñalada mortal. Este hombre es, pues, también un asesino. Pero los Tribunales, naturalmente, no sospechan, ni sospecharán jamás esta tercera mano del ladrón.

En tanto, él sigue ahora de pechos sobre su mosqueada tarima, tara- reando su triste yaraví.

Estoy cárdeno. Mientras me peino, al espejo advierto que mis ojeras se han amoratado aún más, y que sobre los angulosos cobres de mi rostro rasurado se ictericia la tez acerbadamente.

Estoy viejo. Me paso la toalla por la frente, y un rayado horizontal en resaltos de menudos pliegues, acentúase en ella, como pauta de una música fúnebre, implacable....

Estoy muerto.

Mi compañero de celda liase levantado temprano y está preparando el té cargado que solemos tomar cada mañana, con el pan duro de un nuevo sol sin esperanza. Nos sentamos después a la desnuda mesita, donde el desayuno humea melancólico, dentro de dos porcelanas sin plato. Y estas tazas a pie, blanquísimas ellas y tan limpias, este pan aún tibio sobre el breve y arrollado mantel de damasco, todo este aroma matinal y doméstico, me recuerda mi paterna casa, mi niñez santiaguina, aquellos desayunos de ocho y diez hermanos de mayor a menor, como los carrizos de una antara, entre ellos yo, el último de todos, parado junto a la mesa del comedor, engomado y chorreando el cabello que acababa de peinar a la fuerza una de las hermanitas; en la izquierda mano un bizcocho entero ¡había de ser entero! y con la derecha de rosadas falangitas, hurtando a escondidas el azúcar de granito en granito....

¡Ay!, el pequeño que así tomaba el azúcar a la buena madre, quien, luego de sorprenderle, se ponía a acariciarle, alisándole los repulgados golfos frontales:

—Pobrecito mi hijo. Algún día acaso no tendrá a quién hurtarle azúcar, cuando él sea grande, y haya muerto su madre.

Y acababa el primer yantar del día, con dos ardientes lágrimas de madre, que empapaban mis trenzas nazarenas.

MURO OCCIDENTAL

Aquella barba al nivel de la tercera moldura de plomo.

Coro de vientos

Jarales estadizos de julio; viento amarrado a cada peciolo manco del mundo grano que en él gravita. Lujuria muerta sobre lomas onfalóideas de la sierra estival. Espera. No ha de ser. Otra vez cantemos. ¡Oh qué dulce sueño!

Por allí mi caballo avanzaba. A los once años de ausencia, acercábame por fin ese día a Santiago, mi aldea natal. El pobre irracional avanzaba, y yo, desde lo más entero de mi ser hasta mis dedos trabajados, pasando quizá por las mismas riendas asidas, por las orejas atentas de cuadrúpedo y volviendo por el golpeteo de los cascos que fingían danzar en el mismo sitio, en misterioso escarceo tanteador de la ruta y lo desconocido, lloraba por mi madre que muerta dos años antes, ya no habría de aguardar ahora el retorno del hijo descarriado y andariego. La comarca toda, el tiempo bueno, el color de cosechas de la tarde de limón, y también alguna masada que por aquí reconocía mi alma, todo comenzaba a agitarme en nostálgicos éxtasis filiales, y casi podían ajárseme los labios para hozar el pezón eviterno, siempre lácteo de la madre; sí, siempre lácteo, hasta más allá de la muerte.

Con ella había pasado seguramente por allí de niño. Sí. En efecto. Pero no. No fue conmigo que ella viajó por esos campos. Yo era entonces muy pequeño. Fue con mi padre, ¡cuántos años haría de ello! Ufff . . . También fue en julio, cerca de la fiesta de Santiago. Padre y madre iban en sus cabalgaduras; él adelante. El camino real. De repente mi padre que acababa de esquivar un choque con repentino maguey de un meandro:

—Señora . . . ¡Cuidado! . . .

Y mi pobre madre ya no tuvo tiempo, y fue lanzada ¡ay! del arzón de las piedras del sendero. Tornáronla en camilla al pueblo. Yo lloraba mucho por mi madre, y no me decían qué le había pasado. Sanó. La noche del alba de la fiesta, ella estaba ya alegre y reía. No estaba ya en cama, y todo era muy bonito. Yo tampoco lloraba ya por mi madre.

Pero ahora lloraba más recordándola así, enferma, postrada, cuando me quería más y me hacía más cariño y también me daba más bizcochos de bajo de sus almohadones y del cajón del velador. Ahora lloraba más, acercándome a Santiago, donde ya sólo la hallaría muerta, sepulta bajo las mostazas maduras y rumorosas de un pobre cementerio.

Mi madre había fallecido hacía dos años a la sazón. La primera noticia de su muerte recibíla en Lima, donde supe también que papá y mis hermanos habían emprendido viaje a una hacienda lejana de propiedad de un tío nuestro, a efecto de atenuar en lo posible el dolor por tan horrible pérdida. El fundo se hallaba en remontísima región de la montaña, al otro lado del río Marañón. De Santiago pasaría yo hacia allá, devorando inacabables senderos de escarpadas punas y de selvas ardientes y desconocidas.

Mi animal resopló de pronto. Cabillo molido vino en abundancia sobre ligero vientecillo, cegándome casi. Una parva de cebada. Y después perspectivóse Santiago, en su escabrosa meseta, con sus tejados retintos al sol ya horizontal. Y todavía, hacia el lado de oriente, sobre la linde de un promontorio amarillo brasil, se veía el panteón retallado a esa hora por la sexta tintura postmeridiana; y yo ya no podía más, y atroz congoja arrecióme sin consuelo.

A la aldea llegué con la noche. Doblé la última esquina, y, al entrar a la calle en que estaba mi casa, alcancé a ver a una persona sentada a solas en el poyo de la puerta. Estaba sola. Muy sola. Tanto, que, ahogando el duelo místico de mi alma, me dio miedo. También sería por la paz casi inerte con que, engomada por la media fuerza de la penumbra, adosábase su silueta al encalado paramento del muro. Particular revuelo de nervios secó mis lagrimales. Avancé. Saltó del poyo mi hermano mayor, Ángel, y recibióme desvalido entre sus brazos. Pocos días hacía que había venido de la hacienda por causa de negocios.

Aquella noche, luego de una mesa frugal, hicimos vela hasta el alba. Visité las habitaciones, corredores y cuadras de la casa; y Ángel, aún cuando hacía visibles esfuerzos para desviar este afán mío por recorrer el amado y viejo caserón, parecía también gustar de semejante suplicio de quien va por los dominios alucinantes del pasado más mero de la vida.

Por sus pocos días de tránsito en Santiago, Ángel habitaba ahora solo en casa, donde, según él, todo yacía tal como quedara a la muerte de mamá. Referíame también como fueron los días de salud que precedieron a la mortal dolencia, y cómo su agonía. ¡Cuántas veces entonces el abrazo fraterno y escarbó nuestras entrañas y removió nuevas gotas de ternura congelada y de lloro!

—¡Ah, esta despensa, donde le pedían pan a mamá, lloriqueando de engaños!—Y abrí una pequeña puerta de sencillos paneles desvencijados. Como en todas las rústicas construcciones de la sierra peruana, en las que a cada puerta únese casi siempre un poyo, cabe el umbral de la que acababa yo de franquear, hallábase recostado uno, el mismo inmemorial de mi niñez, sin duda, rellenado y enlucido incontables veces. Abierta la humilde portezuela, en él nos sentamos, y allí también pusimos la linterna ojitriste que portábamos. La lumbre de ésta fue a golpear de lleno el rostro de Ángel, que extenuábase de momento en momento, conforme transcurría la noche y reverdecíamos más la herida, hasta parecerme a veces casi transparente. Al advertirle así en tal instante, le acaricié y cubrí de ósculos sus barbadas y severas mejillas que volvieron a empaparse de lágrimas.

Una centella, de esas que vienen de lejos, ya sin trueno, en época de verano en la sierra, le vació las entrañas a la noche. Volví restregándome los párpados a Ángel. Y ni él ni la linterna, ni el poyo, ni nada estaba allí. Tampoco oí ya nada. Sentíme como en una tumba. . . .

Después volvía ver a mi hermano, la linterna, el poyo. Pero creí notarle ahora a Ángel el semblante como refrescado, apacible y quizás me equivocaba—diríase restablecido de su aflicción y flaqueza anteriores. Tal vez, repito, esto era un error de visión de mi parte, ya que tal cambio no se puede ni siquiera concebir.

—Me parece verla todavía—continué sollozando—no sabiendo la pobrecita qué hacer para la dádiva y arguyéndome:—¡Ya te cogí, mentiroso; quieres decir que lloras cuando estás riendo a escondidas! ¡Y me besaba a mí más que a todos ustedes, como yo era el último también!

Al término de la velada de dolor, Ángel parecióme de nuevo muy quebrantado, y, como antes de la centella, asombrosamente descarnado. Sin duda, pues, había yo sufrido una desviación de la vista, motivada por el golpetazo de luz del meteoro, al encontrar antes en su fisonomía un alivio y una lozanía que, naturalmente, no podía haber ocurrido.

Aún no asomaba la aurora del día siguiente, cuando monté y partí para la hacienda, despidiéndome de Ángel que quedaba todavía unos días más, por los asuntos que habían motivado su arribo a Santiago.

Finada la primera jornada del camino, acontecióme algo inaudito. En la posada hallábame reclinado en un poyo descansando, y he aquí que una anciana del bohío, de pronto mirándome asustada, preguntóme lastimera:

—¿Qué le ha pasado, señor, en la cara? ¡Parece que la tiene usted ensangrentada, Dios mío! ...

Salté del asiento. Y al espejo advertíme en efecto el rostro encharcado de pequeñas manchas de sangre reseca. Tuve un fuerte escalofrío, y quise correr de mí mismo. ¿Sangre? ¿De dónde? Yo había juntado el rostro al de Ángel que lloraba.... Pero ... No. No ¿De dónde era esa sangre? Comprenderáse el terror y la alarma que anudaron en mi pecho mil presentimientos. Nada es comparable con aquella sacudida de mi corazón. No habrán palabras tampoco para expresarla ahora ni nunca. Y hoy mismo, en el cuarto solitario donde escribo está la sangre añeja aquella y mi cara en ella untada y la vieja del tambo y la jornada y mi hermano que llora y a quien no besó mi madre muerta y ...

... Al trazar las líneas anteriores he huido disparado a mi balcón, jadeante y sudando frío. Tal es de espantoso y apabullante el recuerdo de esa escarlata misteriosa....

¡Oh noche de pesadilla en esa inolvidable choza, en que la imagen de mi madre muerta alternó, entre forcejeos de extraños hilos, sin punta, que se rompían luego de sólo ser vistos, con la de Ángel, que lloraba rubíes vivos, por siempre jamás!

Seguí ruta. Y por fin, tras una semana de trote por la cordillera y por tierras calientes de montañas, luego de atravesar el Marañón, una mañana entré en parajes de la hacienda. El nublado espacio reverberaba a saltos con lontanos truenos y solanas fugaces.

Desmonté junto al bramadero del portón de la casa que da al camino. Algunos perros ladraron en la calma apacible y triste de la fuliginosa montaña. ¡Después de cuánto tiempo tornaba yo ahora a esa mansión solitaria, enclavada en las quiebras más profundas de las selvas!

Una voz que llamaba y contenía desde adentro a los mastines, entre el alerta gárrulo de las aves domésticas alborotadas pareció ser olfateada extrañamente por el fatigado y tembloroso solípedo que estornudó repetidas veces, enristró casi horizontalmente las orejas hacia delante, y, encabritándose, probó a quitarme los frenos de la mano en son de escape. La enorme portada estaba cerrada. Diríase que toquéla de manera casi maquinal. Luego aquella misma voz siguió vibrando muros adentro, y llegó un instante en que, al desplegarse, con medroso restallido, las gi-

gantescas hojas del portón, ese timbre bucal vino a pararse en mis propios veintiséis años totales y me dejó de punta a la Eternidad. Las puertas
hiciéronse a ambos lados.

¡Meditad brevemente sobre suceso increíble, rompedor de las leyes de
la vida y de la muerte, superador de toda posibilidad; palabra de esperanza y de fe entre el absurdo y el infinito, innegable desconexión de lugar
y de tiempo; nebulosa que hace llorar de inarmónicas armonías incog-
noscibles!

¡Mi madre apareció a recibirme!

—Hijo mío—exclamó estupefacta—. ¿Tú vivo? ¿Has resucitado? ¿Qué
es lo que veo, Señor de los Cielos?

¡Mi madre! ¡Mi madre en alma y cuerpo. Viva! Y con tanta vida, que hoy
pienso que sentí ante su presencia entonces, asomar por las ventanillas
de mi nariz, de súbito, dos desolados granizos de decrepitud que luego
fueron a caer y pesar en mi corazón hasta curvarme senilmente, como si,
a fuerza de un fantástico trueque de destino, acabase mi madre de nacer
y yo viniese, en cambio desde tiempos tan viejos, que me daban una emoción paternal respecto de ella.

Sí. Mi madre estaba allí. Vestida de negro unánime. Viva. Ya no muerta.
¿Era posible? No. No era posible. De ninguna manera. No era mi madre
esa señora. No podía serlo. Y luego ¿qué había dicho al verme? ¿Me creía,
pues, muerto?

—¡Hijo de mi alma!—rompió a llorar mi madre y corrió a estrecharme
contra su seno, con ese frenesí y ese llanto de dicha con que siempre me
amparó en todas mis llegadas y mis despedidas.

Yo habíame puesto como piedra. La vi echarme sus brazos adorados al
cuello, besarme ávidamente y como queriendo devorarme y sollozar sus
mimos y sus caricias que ya nunca volverán a llover en mis entrañas. To-
móme luego bruscamente el impasible rostro a dos manos, miróme así,
cara a cara, acabándome de preguntas. Yo, después de algunos segundos,
me puse también a llorar, pero sin cambiar de expresión ni de actitud: mis
lágrimas parecían agua pura que vertían dos pupilas de estatua.

Por fin enfoqué todas las dispersadas luces de mi espíritu. Retiréme
algunos pasos atrás. E hice entonces comparecer ¡oh, Dios mío! a esa
maternidad a la que no quería recibir mi corazón y la desconocía y le tenía
miedo; las hice comparecer ante no sé qué cuando sacratísimo, desconocido para mí hasta ese momento, y di un grito mudo y de dos filos en toda

su presencia, con el mismo compás del martillo que se acerca y aleja del yunque, con que lanza el hijo su primer quejido, al ser arrancado del vientre de la madre, y con el que parece indicarle que ahí va vivo por el mundo y darle al mismo tiempo, una guía y una señal para reconocerse entrambos por los siglos de los siglos. Y gemí fuera de mí mismo:

—¡Nunca! ¡Nunca! Mi madre murió hace tiempo. No puede ser....

Ella incorporóse espantada ante mis palabras y como dudando de si yo era yo. Volvió a estrecharme entre sus brazos, y ambos seguimos llorando llanto que jamás lloró ni llorará ser vivo alguno.

—Sí—le repetía.—Mi madre murió ya. Mi hermano Ángel también lo sabe.

Y aquí las manchas de sangre que advirtiera en mi rostro, pasaron por mi mente como signos de otro mundo.

—¡Pero hijo de mi corazón!—susurraba casi sin fuerza ella.—¿Tú eres mi hijo muerto y al que yo misma vi en su ataúd? Sí. ¡Eres tú mismo! ¡Creo en Dios! ¡Ven a mis brazos! Pero ¿qué?... ¿No ves que soy tu madre? ¡Mírame! ¡Mírame! ¡Pálpame, hijo mío! ¿Acaso no lo crees?

Contempléla otra vez. Palpé su adorable cabecita encanecida. Y nada. Yo no creía nada.

—Sí, te veo—le respondí—te palpo. Pero no creo. No puede suceder tanto imposible.

¡Y me reí con todas mis fuerzas!

LIBERACIÓN

Ayer estuve en los talleres tipográficos del Panóptico, a corregir unas pruebas de imprenta.

El jefe de ellos es un penitenciado, un bueno, como lo son todos los delincuentes del mundo. Joven, inteligente, muy cortés; Solís, que así se llama el preso, pronto ha hecho grandes inteligencias conmigo, y hame referido su caso, hame expuesto sus quejas, su dolor.

—De los quinientos presos que hay aquí—afirma—, apenas alcanzarán a una tercera parte quienes merezcan ser penados de esta manera. Los demás no; los demás son quizás tan o más morales que los propios jueces que los condenaron.

Arcenan sus ojos el ribete de no sé qué platillo invisible, y de amargura. ¡La eterna injusticia!

Viene hacia mí uno de los obreros. Alto, fornido, acércase como alborozado y me dice:

—Señor, buenas tardes. Cómo está usted—. Y me tiende la mano con viva efusión.

No le reconozco. Le pregunto por su nombre.

—¿No recuerda usted? Soy Lozano. Usted estuvo en la cárcel de Trujillo cuando yo también estuve en ella. Supe que lo absolvió el Tribunal y tuve mucho gusto.

En efecto. Ya le recuerdo. Pobre hombre. Fue condenado a nueve años de penitenciaría, por ser uno de los coautores de un homicidio.

Cuando se aleja de nosotros el atento, Solís me inquiere sorprendido:

—¡Cómo! ¿También usted las había sufrido?

—También—le respondo—; también, amigo mío.

Y le refiero, a mi vez, las circunstancias de mi prisión en Trujillo, procesado por incendio frustrado, robo y asonada. . . .

El sonríe y de nuevo me pregunta:

—Si usted ha estado en Trujillo, debe de haber conocido a Jesús Palomino, oriundo de aquel departamento, que purgó aquí doce años de prisión.

Hago memoria.

—Ahí tiene usted—añade—Aquel hombre era una víctima inocente de la mala organización de la justicia.

Calla breves instantes y, después de mirarme a la cara con mirada escrutadora, prorrumpe resueltamente:

—Voy a contarle a la ligera lo que a Palomino le sucedió aquí.

La tarde está gris y llueve. Las maquinarias y linotipos cuelgan penosos traquidos metálicos en el aire oscuro y arrecido.

Vuelvo los ojos y distingo a lo lejos la cara regordeta de un preso que sonríe bonachonamente entre los aceros negros en movimiento. Es mi peón. El que está compaginando mi obra. Sonríe este desgraciado a toda hora. Diríase que ha perdido el sentimiento verdadero de su infortunio, o que se ha vuelto idiota.

Solís tose, y, con acento trabajoso, empieza su relato:

—Palomino era un hombre bueno. Sucedió que se vio estafado en forma cínica e insultante por un avezado a tales latrocinios, a quien, por ser de la alta sociedad, nunca le castigaron los tribunales. Viéndose, de este modo, a la miseria, y a raíz de un violento altercado entre ambos, sobrevino lo inesperado: un disparo, el muerto, el Panóptico. Luego de recluido aquí, el pobre tuvo que sobrellevar tenebrosa pesadilla. Eso era horroroso. ¡Hasta los mismos que le veíamos, hubimos de sufrir su contagio infernal! ¡Qué atrocidad! Más valiera la muerte. Sí, señor. ¡Más valiera la muerte! ...

El tranquilo narrador quiere llorar. Se nota que revive nítidamente el pasado, pues se le humedecen los ojos, y tienen que callar un instante para no demostrar en la voz que está sollozando en el alma.

—Cuando me acuerdo—agrega—no sé cómo pudo Palomino resistir tanto. Porque aquello era un tormento indescriptible. No sé por qué conducto fue noticiado de que se le tramaba un envenenamiento dentro de la prisión, desde mucho tiempo antes de ser alojado en ella. La familia del hombre que él mató, le perseguía de esta manera hasta más allá de su desgracia. No se contentaba con verle condenado a quince años de penitenciaría y arrastrar a su familia a una ruina clamorosa: llevaba su sed de venganza aun más abajo. Y ahora se embreñaba en recova por tras de los quicios de los sótanos y entre espora y espora de los líquenes que crecen entre los dedos carceleros, tanteando el resorte más secreto de la prisión; ahora se movía aquí, con más libertad que antes a la luz del sol para la injusta sentencia, e hincaba las pestañas de infame emboscada en la atmósfera que había de venir a respirar el condenado. Noticiado éste de ello, sufrió, como usted comprenderá, terrible sorpresa; lo supo, y nada pudo desde entonces ya desvanecérselo. Un hombre de bien, como él, temía una muerte así, no por él, claro, sino por ella y por ellos, la inocente prole atravesada de estigma y orfandad. De allí la zozobra de minuto en minuto y el sobresalto a cada trance de su vida cotidiana. Diez años había pasado así, cuando le vi por primera vez. Despertaba en el ánimo ese atormentado, no ya lástima y compasión, sino un religioso y casi beatífico transporte inexplicable. No daba piedad. Llenaba el corazón de algo quizás más suave y tranquilo y dulce casi. Mirándole, yo no sentía impulsos de deschapar sus hierros, ni de encorecer sus llagas que crecían verdinegras en el fondo de todos sus fondos. Yo no habría hecho nada de esto. Mirando tamaño suplicio, tan sobrehumana actitud de pavor, siempre quise dejarle así, marchar paso a paso, a sobresaltos, a pausas, filo a filo, hacia la encrucijada fatal, hacia la jurada muerte, tanto tiempo ha revelada. No movía Palomino por entonces a socorro. Sólo llenaba el corazón de algo quizás más vago e ideal, más sereno y casi dulce; y era grato, de un agrado misericordioso, dejarle subir su cuesta, dejarle cruzar los pasillos y galerías en penumbra, y entrar y salir por las celdas frías, en su horrendo juego de inestables trapecios, de vuelos de agonía, al acaso, sin punto fijo dónde ir a parar. Con su barba roja a vellones y sus verdes ojos de alga polar, el uniforme estropeado, asustadizo, azorado, parecía atisbarlo todo siempre. Un obstinado gesto de desconfianza resbalaba por sus labios de justo pavorido, por sus cabellos bermejos, por sus sainados pantalones y aun por sus dedos desvalidos, que buscaban en toda la extensión de su capilla de condenado, sin poderlo hallar nunca, un lugar seguro en qué apoyarse. ¡Cuántas veces le vi quizás al borde de la muerte! Un día fue aquí, en la imprenta, durante el trabajo. Callado, meditabundo, taciturno, Palomino hallábase limpiando unas fajas de jebe negro, en un ángulo del taller, y, de cuando en cuando, echaba una mirada recelosa en torno suyo, haciendo girar furtivamente los globos de sus ojos, con el aire visionario de los de una ave nocturna que entreviese fatídicos fantasmas. De repente tuvo un brusco movimiento. Uno de los compañeros de labor, en quien yo había sorprendido repetidas ocasiones marcados gestos y extrañas palabras de sutil aversión, tal vez inmotivada, hacia Palomino, mirábale de hito en hito, desde el lado opuesto de la estancia. Tal conducta, cuya intención no podía, desde luego, serle grata a mi amigo, por los antecedentes que dejo ya anotados, le hizo experimentar un brusco movimiento de desasosiego y agudo escozor destempló todos sus nervios. El gratuito odiador, a su vez, advirtióse sorprendido, y, perdida la serenidad, con torpeza y turbación asaz significativas, vertió de un pequeño frasco de vidrio, algunas gotas; el color y la densidad de éstas fueron envueltas y veladas casi completamente por una alígera voluta de humo que en tal instante venía del lado de los motores. No sé decir dónde fueron a caer esas largas misteriosas lágrimas; pero quien las había vertido siguió agitándose entre los objetos de su trabajo, cada vez con más visible turbación, hasta el punto de no tener posiblemente conciencia de lo que hacía. Palomino le observaba estático, sobrecogido de presentimiento, con las pupilas fijas, pendientes de aquella maniobra que inspirábale intensa expectación y angustiosa zozobra. Luego las manos del trabajador fueron a ensamblar un lingote de plomo entre otras barras dispuestas en la mesa de labor. Entonces Palomino cesa de aguaitarle, y, atónito, abstraído, bajos los ojos, superpone círculos con la fantasía herida de sospecha, desembroca afinidades, vuelve a sorprender nudos, a enjaezar intenciones fatales y rematar siniestras escaleras. . . . Otro día ingresó de la calle una desconocida visita, la cual acercóse al linotipista y le habló largo rato; no se percibían sus palabras entre el ruido de los talleres. Palomino saltó, plantóle la vista, analizándole de pies a cabeza, a hurtadillas, pálido de temor. . . . "¡Palomino! ¡Vea!" —le consolaba yo— "Olvide usted eso; creo que no puede ser." Y él, por toda respuesta, apoyaba las sienes entre ambas manos, tintas de encierro y desamparo, vencido, sin fuerzas. A los pocos meses de habérseme traído aquí, él era mi mejor amigo, el más leal, el más bueno.

Solís se emociona visiblemente y yo también.

—¿Tiene usted frío?—me interroga con súbita ternura.

Hace rato, sin duda, la estancia está llena de una neblina densa que azulea en extraños cendales en torno a las ampolletas de luz roja. Por los altos ventanales vese que sigue lloviendo. Hace mucho frío en verdad.

Suenan como entre apretados algodones impregnados de limalla de hielo, notas dispersas de un solfeo distante. Es la banda de músicos de la Penitenciaría que ensayan el himno del Perú. Suenan esas notas, y desusada sugestión ejercen ahora en mi espíritu, hasta el punto de casi sentir la letra misma de la canción, engarzada sílaba por sílaba, o como clavada con gigantescos clavos en cada uno de los sonidos errantes.

Las notas se cruzan, se iteran, patalean, chirrían, vuelven a iterarse, destrozan tímidos biseles.

—¡Ah, qué suplicio el de aquel hombre!—exclama el preso con creciente lástima. Y continúa narrando entre silencios continuos, durante los cuales sin duda trata de atrapar los tremendos recuerdos:

—Era una obsesión indestructible la suya, cimentada sabe Dios por quién, para no caer nunca. Muchos decían: "Está loco Palomino." ¡Loco! ¿Puede acaso estar loco quien en circunstancias normales, cuida de su existencia en peligro? ¿Y puede estarlo quien, sufriendo los zarpazos del odio, aun con la complicidad misma de la justicia, precave aquel peligro y trata de pararlo con todas sus fuerzas exacerbadas de hombre que lo cree posible todo, por propia experiencia de dolor? ¡Loco! ¡No! ¡Demasiado cuerdo quizá! ¿Quién, con qué formidable persuasión, sobre cuáles incuestionables visos de posibilidad, habíale infundido tal idea? A pesar de haberme expuesto Palomino muchas veces los torvos alambres ocultos que, según él, podrían vibrar desde fuera hasta el hilo de su existencia, difícil me era ver claramente aquel peligro. "Como usted no conoce a esos malvados," . . . refunfuñaba impertérrito Palomino. Yo, luego de argumentarle cuanto podía, me callaba. "Me escriben de mi casa—díjome otro día—y vuelven a dármelo a entender; puede venir pronto mi indulto, y pagarían cualquier precio por evitar mi salida. Sí. Hoy más que nunca, el peligro está a mi lado, amigo mío. . . ." Y sus últimas palabras ahogáronle en desgarradores sollozos. La verdad es que, ante la constante desesperación de Palomino, llegué a sufrir, a veces, sobre todo en los últimos tiempos, repentinas y profundas crisis de duda, admitiendo la posibilidad de cualquiera alevosía, aun de la más negra para su vida, y llegué hasta a asegurárselo, a mi vez, a los demás amigos de la prisión, alegándoles, probándoles por medio de no sé qué insospechados aportes de peso decisivo, la sensatez con que razonaba Palomino. Más todavía. Hubo ocasiones en que ya no era duda lo que yo sentía, sino seguridad incontrovertible del peligro, y yo mismo salíale al encuentro con nuevas sospechas y vehementes advertencias de mi parte, sobre el horror de lo que podía sobrevenir, y esto lo hacía precisamente cuando él se hallaba tranquilo, en algún olvido visionario. Diríase, que entonces era en mí en quien se había metido el terror más adentro que en él mismo. Yo le quería mucho, es cierto; yo me interesaba intensamente por su situación, siempre de pie a la cabecera de su espanto; y de tácito modo le ayudaba a escudriñar los cárabos de su pesadilla; en fin, yo llegué por último, a registrar de hecho los bolsillos y los menores actos de numerosos compañeros y empleados del establecimiento, tanteando el escondido pelo de su tragedia inminente. . . . Todo esto es verdad. Pero también verá usted, por cuanto le refiero, que, a fuerza de interesarme tanto por Palomino, iba convirtiéndome en su propio torturador, en un verdadero verdugo suyo. "¡Tenga usted cuidador—le decía yo con agorera angustia. Palomino daba un salto, y trémulo volvíase a todos lados y quería huir sin saber por dónde. Y ambos experimentábamos entonces, acerba, terrible desesperación, vallados por los muros de piedra, invulnerables, implacables, absolutos, eternos. Palomino, desde luego, no comía casi. Cómo iba a comer. No bebía. No hubiera respirado. En cada migaja veía latente el veneno mortal. En cada gota de agua. En cada adarme de la atmósfera. Su tenaz escrupulosidad sutilizada hasta la hiperestesia, le hacía parecer los más triviales movimientos ajenos, relacionados con los alimentos. Alguien, cierta mañana, comía a su lado, pan del bolsillo. Palomino vióle llevarse a los labios el mendrugo, y, tras una enérgica mueca de repulsa, escupió varias veces y fue a enjuagarse. "¡Tenga usted siempre cuidado"!—le repetía yo cada día con más frecuencia. Dos, cuatro veces diarias este alerta resonaba entre ambos. Yo me desahogaba, sabiendo que de este modo, Palomino se cuidaría más y alejaríase mejor del peligro. Me parecía, en fin, que cuando yo no le había recordado mucho rato la fatídica inquietud, él podría acaso olvidarla y entonces ¡ay de él! . . . ¿Dónde estaba Palomino? . . . Pues, llevado por mi vigilante fraternidad, de un salto llegábame a él, y le susurraba al oído atropelladamente: "¡Tenga usted cuidado! . . ." Así me tranquilizaba yo, pues podía estar cierto de que en algunas horas no le sucedería nada a mi amigo. Un día se lo repetí más a menudo que nunca. Palomino oíame, y, luego de la conmoción consiguiente, de seguro me lo agradecía en su pensamiento y en su corazón. Mas, tengo que volver a recordárselo a usted; por este camino traspasaba las lindes del amor y del bien por Palomino y me convertía en su principal tormento; en su propio verdugo. Yo me daba cuenta de este doble valor de mi conducta. Pero—me decía yo allá en mi conciencia—sea lo que fuere: irrevocable imperativo de mi alma, me ha investido de guardián suyo, de curador de su seguridad, y no volveré atrás por nada. Mi voz de alerta palpitaría siempre al lado suyo, en su noche de zozobra, como un despertador para el escudo y la defensa. Sí. Yo no volvería atrás, por nada. Una media noche, desperté sobresaltado, a consecuencia de haber sentido en mitad del sueño, un vivo espanto misterioso. Tal una válvula abierta de golpe, que me arrojara en todo el pecho un golpe de agua fresca. Desperté, poseído de gran alegría, de una alada alegría, cual si de pronto me hubiera abandonado un formidable peso agobiador, o hubiera saltado de mi cuello una horca, hecha pedazos. Era una alegría ciega, de no sé por qué; y a tientas desperezábase y aleteaba en mi corazón, diáfana, pura. Desperté bien. Hice conciencia. Cesó mi alegría: había soñado que Palomino era envenenado. A la mañana siguiente, el sueño aquel me tenía sobrecogido, con crecientes palpitaciones de encrucijada: la muerte—la vida. Sentíame en realidad totalmente embargado por él. Ásperos vientos de enervante fiebre, corríanme el pulso, las sienes, el pecho. Debía yo demostrar aire de enfermo, sin duda, pues harto me pesaban las sienes, la cabeza y velaban mi ánima graves pesares. Por la tarde, a Palomino y a mí tocónos trabajar juntos en la Imprenta. Como ahora, los aceros negros rebullían, chocaban cual reprochándose, rozábanse y se salvaban a las ganadas, giraban quizás locamente, con más velocidad que nunca. Durante toda la mañana y hasta la tarde, el sueño aquel acompañóme terco, irreductible. Mas, ignoro por qué, yo no lo rehuía. Lo sentía a mi lado, riendo y llorando alternativamente, enseñándome, sin son ni ton, una de sus manos, la siniestra, negra; blanca, bien blanquísima la otra, y ambas entrelazándose siempre con extraño isocronismo, en impecable, aterradora encrucijada; ¡la muerte—la vida! ¡la vida—la muerte! Durante todo el día también—y también ignoro por qué—ni una sola vez acudió a mis labios el velador alerta de antes. Absolutamente. Mi sueño anterior parecía sellar mi boca para no verter tal palabra, por su propia diestra albicante y luminosa, de una luminosidad azul, esfumada, sin bordes. De repente, Palomino murmuró a mis oídos, con contenida explosión de lástima e impotencia: "Tengo sed." Inmediatamente, empujado por mi solícita hermandad de siempre para con él, apresté una escudilla de greda rojiza, y en ella fui a traerle a que bebiese. El agradeció enternecido, asiéndose del asa de la vasija, y sació su sed hasta que ya no pudo. . . . Y al crepúsculo, cuando esta vida de punzantes cuidados hacíase más insoportable; cuando Palomino habíase agujereado ya toda la cabeza, a punta de zozobras; cuando febril amarillez de un amarillo de nuevo viejo, aplácabale el rostro desorbitado de inquietud; cuando hasta el médico mismo declarado había que aquel mártir no tenía nada más que debilidad, motivada por malestar del estómago; cuando estaba ya añicos ese uniforme sainado de excesiva, cediza agonía; cuando hasta Palomino había esbozado ¡oh armonía secreta de los cielos! a la vera de las arrugas de su propia frente, fugitiva sonrisa alta, que no alcanzó a saltar a las bajas mejillas, ni a la humana tristeza de sus hombros; y cuando, como hoy, llovía y había neblina por los libres espacios inalcanzables, y arreciaba por aquí abajo un premioso y hosco augurio sin causa ... al crepúsculo, acercóse él y me dijo, a sangrantes astillas de voz: "¡Solís ... Solís.... Ya ... ya me mataron! ... Solís ..." Al verle ambas manos sosteniéndose el vientre y retorciéndose de dolor, sentí, antes que en el fondo de mi corazón, caerme el golpe, en sensación de fuego devorador y crepitante, dentro de mis propias vísceras integrales. Sus quejas, apenas articuladas, como no queriendo fuesen percibidas más que por mí solo, soplaban hacia mi interior, como avivadas lenguas de una llama mucho tiempo atrás contenida entre los dos, en forma de invisibles comprimidos. ¡De tan seguro modo, con tan viva certidumbre habíamos ambos por igual, esperado aquel desenlace! Mas, luego de sentir como si el áspid hubiérase colado por las venas de mi propio cuerpo, invadióme instantánea, súbita, misteriosa satisfacción ¡Misteriosa satisfacción! ¡Sí señor! ...

En esto, Solís hizo una mueca de enigmática ofuscación, mezclada de tan sorda ebriedad en la mirada, que me hizo bambolear en el asiento, como con una pedrada furibunda.

Después, enronquecido, a pulso, a grandes toneladas, agregó misteriosamente:

—Y Palomino no amaneció al siguiente día. ¿Había, pues, sido envenenado? ¿Y acaso con el agua que yo le di a beber? ¿O había sido aquello sólo un acceso nervioso suyo y nada más? No lo sé. Sólo dicen que al otro día, mientras yo vime obligado a guardar cama en las primeras horas, a causa de los fuertes golpes nerviosos de la víspera; dicen que entonces vino un hijo suyo a noticiar a su padre habérsele concedido el indulto, y ya no le encontró. Le había respondido la Dirección del establecimiento: "En efecto. Concedido el indulto para su padre, ha sido puesto en libertad esta mañana."

El narrador tuvo en esto un mal contenido gesto de tormento que me impulsó a decirle, solícito y consternado:

—No ... No ... ¡No vaya usted a llorar!

Y, haciendo súbito paréntesis, volvió Solís a preguntarme con honda ternura, como antes:

—¿Tiene usted frío?

Yo le interrumpo anhelante:

—¿Y después?

—Y después... nada.

Y luego, Solís calló hasta la muerte. Y luego, como cosa aparte, lleno de amor y amargura a un tiempo, añadió:

—Pero Palomino, que ha sido siempre un hombre bueno y mi mejor amigo, el más leal, el más bondadoso; a quien yo quería tanto, por cuya situación me interesaba intensamente, a quien le ayudé a escudriñar su futuro amenazado, y por quien llegué hasta registrar de hecho los bolsillos y los actos de los demás; Palomino no ha vuelto más por aquí, ni se acuerda de mí. Es un ingrato. ¡Qué le parece!

Se oye de nuevo a la banda de músicos de la Penitenciaría tocar el himno del Perú. Ahora ya no solfean. El coro de la canción es tocado por toda la banda y en su integral sinfonía. Suenan las notas de ese himno, y el preso que permanece en silencio, sumido en sus hondas cavilaciones, agita de pronto los párpados en vivo aleteo y exclama con gesto alucinado:

—¡Es el himno el que tocan! ¿Lo oye usted? Es el himno. ¡Qué claro! Parece hacerse lenguas:

Soo-mos-liii-bres....

Y al tararear estas notas, sonríe y ríe por fin con absurda alegría.

Luego vuelve a la reja inmediata los encandilados ojos, en los que está brillando un brillo de lágrimas ardidas. Salta del asiento, y, tendiendo los brazos, exclama con júbilo que me estremece hasta los huesos:

—¡Hola Palomino!...

Alguien avanza hacia nosotros, a través de la cerrada verja silente e inmóvil.

Sí. Conocí al hombre a quien luego aconteció mucho acontecimiento. Tanto tuvo, pues, haberme ido en lo sucedido a aquel sujeto, en verdad, siempre digno de curiosidad y holgadas meditaciones, a causa del aire de espantadiza irregularidad de su modo de ser. . . . La ciudad le tenía por loco, idiota o poco menos. A ser franco, diré que yo nunca le tuve en igual concepto. Yerro. Sí le tuve como anormal, pero sólo en virtud de poseer un talento grandeocéano y una auténtica sensibilidad de poeta.

Cierta vez hasta almorzamos juntos en el hotel. Otra vez comimos. Y tomamos desayuno otro día. Y así durante cuatro o cinco meses seguidos, que vivió solo, por ausencia de los suyos del lugar. Lato humor el de nuestra mesa. Hasta las finas lozas pálidas y los cristales, sonríen con brillo inteligente en su límpida dentadura de turno. Un charlador endemoniado el señor Marcos Lorenz. Yo estaba lindo. A poco le llegué a tener cariño y a extrañarle harto, cuando faltaba al restorán.

El señor Lorenz era soltero y no tenía hijo alguno. A la sazón contaba diez años, como enamorado de una aristocrática dama de la ciudad. Diez años. No sonriáis. Sí. El señor Lorenz amaba a su amada hacía una década. El mismo habíamelo declarado, así como también que ella, a pesar de no haber estado juntos jamás, lo sabía todo, y quizá, a su vez, le amaba un tanto, pues el señor Lorenz la escribía su cariño a menudo. Viejo amor flamante siempre aquél, vibrando día tras día, desde el mismo traste, desde el mismo sostenido en sí bemol, hasta haberse evado en todos los oídos del distrito, donde nadie ignoraba semejante historia neoplatónica, a la que, desde la primera a la última página, exornaba un texto igual, con sólo ligeras variaciones tipográficas y, posiblemente, hasta gramaticales. ¡Viejo amor flamante siempre aquél!

—¡Acaso me ama un poco!—repetíase en la mesa el señor Lorenz, ovalando un mordisco episcopal sobre el sabroso choclo de mayo, que deshacíase y lactaba, de puro tierno, entre los cuatro dígitos del tenedor argénteo. Porque, en verdad, mi excelente contertulio no parecía estar muy seguro de lo que sentiría por él la dama de su corazón. Tanto, que muchas veces, su tranquilidad ante esta incertidumbre, y la longevidad de semejantes relaciones estadizas, tornábanme descreído, y hacíanme pensar que todo no podía pasar acaso de un reverendísimo boato de vanidad inofensiva, de parte del señor Lorenz, ya que él era apenas un ciudadano más o menos herbolario, y ella un divino anélido de miel, hecho para volverle agua la boca al más ahíto de los salomones de la tierra. Mas vino prueba en contrario, una mañana en que ingresó el señor Lorenz al restorán. ¿Qué le pasaba al señor Lorenz? ¿Qué cara traía, tan a crespas facciones trabajada?

—¿Algún borrón en la tela, amigo mío?

—Nada—respondióme en un mugido—Sólo que acaba de pasar ella, acompañada de un bribón, de quien ya me han noticiado como novio suyo....

—¿Cómo?—aducíle sarcásticamente—¿Y usted? ¿Y sus diez años de amor?

El señor Lorenz salióme entonces al encuentro, pidiendo un antipasto de jamón del país y sardinas. Servido éste, añadió regocijado:

—Parece estar mejor que el de ayer.

Y, como si se vendase una ligera picazón de insecto, voceó:

—¡Mozo! ¡Whisky!

No obstante lo cual, notificado quedaba yo, con roja cédula de celos, que, verdaderamente, lo que el señor Lorenz sentía por aquella dama, era una pasión a todo cuadrante. No cabía duda. ¡Viejo amor flamante siempre el suyo!

Una tarde leí, poco después, en uno de los diarios locales:

Enlace concertado.—Ha quedado concertado el enlace del señor Walter Wolcot, con la señorita Nérida del Mar.

¡Pesia! ¡Pobre señor Lorenz! Qué amargas calabazas le florecían. Calabazas decenarias. Aquel divino anélido de miel iba a subjuntivar su áureo nombre aqueo, al rápido de trusts del bribón de quien ya habían noticiado al señor Lorenz, como prometido de Nérida.

Terrible pesar sobrevino a mi amigo, como podrá suponerse, ante el anuncio de aquel matrimonio. Acabáronse las sobremesas plácidas; y las aguas de oro y los espumosos benedictines de antes, quizás sólo lloraban ahora, estancados en las pupilas de este nuevo José Matías, que, desde entonces, parecía estar siempre pronto a verter lágrimas de desesperación. Acabóse el buen humor que arcenara, en jocunda guardilla tornasol, la fraternal efusión de los almuerzos soleados y las florecidas cenas retardadas: pues, aun cuando el apetito por las buenas viandas arreciaba con fuerza mayor en el señor Lorenz, a raíz de su sétima caída romántica, quijarudo Pierrot punteaba ahora en su alma herida, ahora que los días y las noches le aporreaban con ocasos moscardados de recuerdos, y lunas amarillas de saudad.

No volvió el señor Lorenz a decir palabra alguna sobre Nérida. Caviloso, callado, sólo de vez en tarde, enventanaba la taciturnidad del yantar, para estornudar algún versículo del Eclesiastés, entre cuyas cenizas aventaba, con aire confinado de orfandad, su desventura. Ante éste, que podría llamarse trágico palimpsesto de amor, tenté, en más de una ocasión, escarbar el secreto de sus pensares, a fin de ver si en algo podría yo aliviarle. Pero nada. Siempre que resolvíame a interrogarle, sentía al hombre trancarse a piedra y lacre, pecho adentro, para toda pregunta o confidencia.

Luego, dos mil ciento sesentidós horas.

Y un domingo al medio día, la orquesta lanza una torreada marcha nupcial, entre las pilastras de rancias molduras provinciales, y bajo los domos iluminados del templo, cuyo altar mayor resplandece enguirnaldado de albos azahares goteantes de campo y de rocío.

Veíase, por la pompa del cortejo, que eran Nérida y el señor Walter Wolcot, quienes, en tales instantes, recibían la bendición del Todopoderoso, en matrimonio; y que, a un tiempo mismo, el destino del muy amado señor Lorenz, calados el lúgubre clac de unto y los guantes negros, asistía al sepelio de diez sarcófagos ingrávidos, en cuyos labrados campos de azabache, habrían, decorados a la usanza etrusca, verdes ramas de miosotys florecido portadas por piérides mútilas y suplicantes; boscajes de rumorosas uvas vivas, bajo el cielo de puras anilinas anacreónticas; vientos encontrados desnudando árboles de otoño; y montañas de hielos eternos. Dentro de los diez sarcófagos, irían diez relojes difuntos. . . .

Y todo era así, en verdad. Los novios eran Nérida y el caballero de la cuádruple V: él, calvete prematuro, sanguinoso tipo congestionado de clubman empedernido que duerme hasta las tres de la tarde; grandes ojos engallados verdebotella, crónico gesto placentero, como si siempre estuviese celebrando algo; flamante traje de una cuasi mortuoria corrección británica. Ella . . . visiblemente pálida.

¿Y el otro? . . . ¡Oh espectáculo de impiedad y de heroísmo! El señor

Marcos Lorenz también estaba allí. Le hallé alarmantemente demudado. El, a su vez, me vio, pero no pareció verme. Le saludé con una venia, y no me hizo caso. Muy cerca de la pareja, erguíase aquel hombre, rígido, petrificado en dantesca lacería.

Monseñor, revestido de finísima pelliza de gran tono, mayaba, con voz enronquecida, el sagrado latín del sacramento. En los incensarios de plata antigua y cadenillas de oro, ardían los granos de resinas místicas. La orquesta por segunda vez doblaba la llave del sol de la partitura; y, sudoroso, el acólito, murmuraba como en sueños, de capítulo en capítulo sus sílabas rituales.

De súbito, la triste desposanda hizo una extraña cosa. En el preciso momento en que el tonsurado la hacía la pregunta de promesa, alzó ella sus ardientes ojos de ámbar oscuro, inundados en febril humedad, y derecho fue a clavarlos en el otro, en el señor Lorenz. Tal, distraída por entero, no contesta. Algunos del cortejo, notan el inesperado silencio, y, siguiendo la dirección de la mirada de Nérida, la encontraron posada en el pobre José Matías. Y luego, todo como en la duración del relámpago, el señor Lorenz recibió aquella mirada, quebró bruscamente su rigidez tormentosa, de un solo tranco lanzóse hacia Nérida, arrollando a cuantos tropezó a su paso, y, con increíble destreza de ave rapaz, cogióla el rostro estupefacto, y la dio un beso furioso en toda su boca virgen, que entreabrióse como un surco.... Luego, el señor Lorenz cayó pesadamente a tierra.

Un revuelo de voces y una repentina parálisis en todos. Y quienes, en son de airada indignación, acercáronse al yacente besador, al inicuo intruso, oreja en pecho oyeron a la Muerte fatigada y sudorosa sentarse a descansar en el corazón ya helado de aquel hombre. ¡Pobre señor Lorenz! Sólo de esta manera, y en sólo este beso fugaz, frotado y encendido por el total de su vida, en la muerte, logró unir su carne a la carne de su amada, que ¡ay! acaso no le había amado nunca en este mundo.

El desposorio quedó frustrado. Ciega polvareda interpúsose, a gran espesor, entre los que hubieran sido esposos. Nérida también había sufrido en tal instante, seria conmoción nerviosa, y, llevada al lecho de dolor, agravándose fue de segundo en segundo, para morir una hora después de la instantánea muerte del pobre José Matías....

Y hoy, corridos ya algunos años, desde que abandonaran el mundo aquellas dos almas, en esta dorada mañana de enero, un niño fino y bello acaba de detenerse en la esquina de Belén, un niño extrañamente hermoso y melancólico.

Pasa un ómnibus del cual bajan varios pasajeros. A uno de ellos, señorón de amplio aire mundano, se le cae el bastón. El niño, tan bello y, sobre todo, tan melancólico, gana a recoger la caída caña, enjoyada de oro rojo casi sangre, y se la entrega al dueño que no es otro sino el propio señor Walter Wolcot. Este advierte el rostro del pequeño, y sin saber por qué, sufre fuerte sobresalto. Vacila. Tartamudo agradece, por fin, la gentileza anónima, y, con desesperada vehemencia que lagrimea de misteriosa inquietud, pregunta al niño:

— ¿Cómo te llamas?

El infante no responde.

— ¿Dónde vives?

El infante no responde.

— ¿Cuántos años tienes?

El infante no responde nada.

— ¿Tus padres? ...

El niño se pone a llorar. ...

Una mosca negra y fatigada viene y trata de posarse en la frente del señor Walter Wolcot, a punto en que éste se aleja del niño. Muy distante ya, se la espanta varias veces.

Luis Urquizo lanzó una carcajada, y, tragándose todavía las últimas pólvoras de risa, bebió ávidamente su cerveza. Luego, al poner el cristal vacío sobre el zinc del mostrador, lo quebró, vociferando:

—¡Eso no es nada! Yo he cabalgado varias veces sobre el lomo de mi caballo que caminaba con sus cuatro cascos negros invertidos hacia arriba. ¡Oh, mi soberbio alazán! Es el paquidermo más extraordinario de la tierra. Y más que cabalgarlo así sorprende, maravilla, hace temblar de pavor el espectáculo en seco, simple y puro de líneas y movimientos que ofrece aquel potro cuando está parado, en imposible gravitación hacia la superficie inferior de un plano suspendido en el espacio. Yo no puedo contemplarlo así, sin sentirme alterado y sin dejar de huir de su presencia, despavorido y como acuchillada la garganta. ¡Es brutal! Parece entonces una gigantesca mosca asida a una de esas vigas desnudas que sostienen los techos humildes de los pueblos ¡Eso es maravilloso! ¡Eso es sublime! ¡Irracional!

Luis Urquizo habla y se arrebata, casi chorreando sangre el rostro rasurado, húmedos los ojos. Trepida; guillotina sílabas, suelda y enciende adjetivos; hace de jinete, depone algunas fintas; conifica en álgidas interjecciones las más anchas sugerencias de su voz, gesticula, iza el brazo, ríe: es patético, es ridículo: sugestiona y contagia en locura.

Después dijo:

—Me marcho—Y corriendo, saltó el dintel de la taberna y desapareció rápidamente

—¡Pobre!—exclamaron todos—. Está completamente loco.

Urquizo, en verdad, estaba desequilibrado. No cabía duda. Así lo confirmaba el curso posterior de su conducta. Aquel hombre continuó viendo las cosas al revés, trastrocándolo todo, a través de los cinco cristales ahumados de sus sentidos enfermos. Las buenas gentes de Cayna, pueblo de su residencia, hicieron de él, como es natural, blanco de cruel curiosidad y cotidiana distracción de grandes y pequeños.

Años más tarde, Urquizo, por falta de cura oportuna, agravóse en forma mortal en su demencia, y llegó al más truculento y edificante diorama del hombre que tiene el triángulo de dos ángulos, que se muerde el codo, que ríe ante el dolor, y llora ante el placer: Urquizo llegó a errar allende las comisuras eternas, a donde corren a agruparse, en son de armonía y plenitud, los siete tintes céntricos del alma y del color.

Por entonces, yo le encontré una tarde. Desde que le avisté, pocos pasos antes de cruzarnos, despertóse en mí desusada piedad hacia aquel desgraciado, que, por lo demás, era primo mío en no sé qué remota línea de consanguinidad materna; y, al cederle la vereda, saludándole de paso, tropecéme en uno de los baches de la empedrada calle, y fui a golpear con el mío un antebrazo del enfermo. Urquizo protestó colérico:

—¡Quía! ¿Está usted loco?

La exclamación sarcástica del alienado me hizo reír; y más adelante fue ella motivo de constantes cavilaciones en que los misterios de la razón se hacían espinas, y empozábanse en el cerrado y tormentoso círculo de una lógica fatal, entre mis sienes. ¿Por qué esa forma de inducción para atribuirme la descompaginación de tornillos y motores que sólo en él había?

Este último síntoma, en efecto, traspasaba ya los límites de la alucinación sensorial. Esto era ya más trascendental, sin duda, desde que representaba, nada menos que un raciocinio, un atar de cabos profundos, un dato de conciencia. Urquizo debía, pues, creerse a sí mismo en sus cabales; debía de estar perfectamente seguro de ello, y, desde este punto de vista suyo, era yo, por haberle golpeado sin motivo, el verdadero loco. Urquizo atravesaba por este plano de juicio normal que se denuncia en casi todos los alienados; plano que, por su desconcertante ironía, hiere y escarnece los riñones más cuerdos, hasta quitarnos toda rienda mental y barrer con todos los hitos de la vida. Por eso, la zurda exclamación de aquel enfermo clavóse tanto en mi alma y todavía me hurga el corazón.

Luis Urquizo pertenecía a una numerosa familia del lugar. Era, por infortunado, muy querido de los suyos, quienes le prestaban toda suerte de cuidados y amorosa asistencia.

Un día se me notificó una cosa terrible. Todos los parientes de Urquizo, que convivían con él, también estaban locos. Y todavía más. Todos ellos eran víctimas de una obsesión común, de una misma idea, zoológica, grotesca, lastimosa, de un ridículo fenomenal; se creían monos, y como tales vivían.

Mi madre invitóme una noche a ir con ella a saber del estado de los parientes locos. No encontramos en la casa de éstos sino a la madre de Urquizo, quien cuando llegamos, se entretenía en hojear tranquilamente un cartapacio de papeluchos, a la luz de la lámpara que pendía en el centro de la sala. Dado el aislamiento y atraso de aquel pueblo, que no poseía instituciones de beneficencia, ni régimen de policía, esos pobres enfermos de la sien salían cuando querían a la calle; y así era de verlos a toda hora cruzar por doquiera la población, introducirse a las casas, despertando siempre la risa y la piedad en todos.

La madre de los alienados, apenas nos divisó, chilló agudamente, frunció las cejas con fuerza y con cierta ferocidad, siguió haciéndolas vibrar de abajo arriba varias veces, arrojó luego con mecánico ademán el pliego que manoseaba; y, acurrucándose sobre la silla, con infantil rapidez de escolar que se enseria ante el maestro, recogió los pies, dobló las rodillas hasta la altura del nacimiento del cuello, y, desde esta forzada actitud, parecida a la de las momias, esperó a que entrásemos a la casa, clavándonos, cabrilleantes, móviles, inexpresivos, selváticos, sus ojos entelarañados que aquella noche suplantaban asombrosamente a los de un mico. Mi madre asióse a mí asustada y trémula, y yo mismo sentíme sobrecogido de espeluznante sensación de espanto. La loca parecía furiosa.

Pero no. A la brusca claridad de la cercana lámpara, distinguimos que aquella cara extraviada, bajo la corta cabellera que le caía en crinejas asquerosas hasta los ojos, empezaba luego a fruncirse y moverse sobre el miserable y haraposo tronco, volviéndose a todos lados, como solicitada por invisibles resortes o por misteriosos ruidos producidos en los ferrados barrotes de un parque. La loca, después, como si prescindiera de nosotros, empezó a rascarse y espulgarse el vientre, los costados, los brazos, triturando los fantásticos parásitos con sus dientes amarillos. De breve en breve chillaba largamente, escrutaba en torno suyo y aguaitaba a la puerta, como si no nos advirtiera. Madre, transcurridos algunos minutos de expectación y de miedo, hízome señas de retroceder, y abandonamos la casa.

De esta lúgubre escena hacía veintitrés años cumplidos, cuando después de haber vivido, separado de los míos durante todo aquel tracto de tiempo, por razón de mis estudios en Lima, tornaba yo una tarde a Cayna, aldea que, por lo solitaria y lejana era como una isla allende las montañas solas. Viejo pueblo de humildes agricultores, separado de los grandes focos civilizados del país por inmensas y casi inaccesibles cordilleras, vivía a menudo largos períodos de olvido y de absoluta incomunicación con las demás ciudades del Perú.

Debo llamar la atención hacia la circunstancia asaz inquietante de no haber tenido noticias de mi familia, en los seis últimos años de mi ausencia.

Mi casa estaba situada casi a la entrada de la población. Un acanelado poniente de mayo, de esos dulces y cogitabundos ponientes del oriente peruano, abríase de brazos sobre la aldea que no sé por qué tenía a esa hora, en su soledad y abandono exteriores, cargado olor a desventura, tenaz aire de lástima. Tal una roña de descuido y destrucción inexplicable rezumaba de todas partes. Ni un solo transeúnte. Y apenas crucé las primeras esquinas, opacáronse mis nervios, golpeados por una súbita impresión de ruina; y sin darme cuenta, estuve a punto de llorar.

El portón lacre y rústico de la mansión familiar apareció abierto de par en par. Descendí de la cabalgadura, y, jadeante de lacerada ternura, torpe de presagiosa emoción, hablando al sudoroso lento animal, avancé zaguán adentro. Inmediatamente, entre el ruido de los cascos, despertáronse en el interior destemplados gritos guturales, como de enfermos que ululasen en medio del delirio y la fatiga.

No podré ahora precisar la suerte de pétreas cadenas que, anillándose en mis costados, en mis sienes, en mis muñecas, en mis tobillos, hasta echarme sangre, mordiéronme con fieras dentelladas, cuando percibí aquella especie de doméstica jauría. La antropoidal imagen de la madre de Urquizo surgió instantáneamente en mi memoria, al mismo tiempo que invadíame un presentimiento tan superior a mis fuerzas que casi me valía por una aciaga certeza de lo que, breves minutos después, había de dar con todo mi ser en la tiniebla.

A toda voz llamé casi gimiendo.

Nada. Todas las puertas de las habitaciones estaban, como la de la calle, abiertas hasta el tope. Solté la brida de mi caballo, corrí de corredor en corredor, de patio en patio, de aposento en aposento, de silencio en silencio; y nuevos gruñidos detuviéronme por fin, delante de una gradería de argamasa que ascendía al granero más elevado y sombrío de la casa. Atisbé. Otra vez se hizo el misterio.

Ninguna seña de vida humana; ni un solo animal doméstico. Extrañas manos debían de haber alterado, con artimañoso desvío del gusto y de todo sentido de orden y comodidad, la usual distribución de los muebles y de los demás enseres y menaje del hogar.

Precipitadamente, guiado por secreta atracción, salté los peldaños de esa escalera; y, al disponerme a trasponer la portezuela del terrado, la advertí franca también. Detúvome allí inexplicable y calofriante tribulación; dudé por breves segundos, y, favorecido por los destellos últimos del día, avizoré ávidamente hacia adentro.

Rabioso hasta causar horror, desnaturalizado hasta la muerte, relampagueó un rostro macilento y montaraz entre las sombras de esa cueva. Enristrando todo mi coraje—¡pues que ya lo suponía todo, Dios mío!— me parapeté junto al marco de la puerta y esforcéme en reconocer esa máscara terrible.

¡Era el rostro de mi padre!

¡Un mono! Sí. Toda la trunca verticalidad y el fácil arresto acrobático; todo el juego de nervios. Toda la pobre carnación facial y la gesticulación; la osamenta entera. Y, hasta el pelaje cosquilleante, ¡oh la lana sutilísima con que está tramada la inconsútil membrana de justo, matemático espesor suficiente que el tiempo y la lógica universal ponen, quitan y trasponen entre columna y columna de la vida en marcha!

—Khirrrrr... Khirrrrr...—silbó trémulamente.

Puedo asegurar que por su parte él no me reconocía. Removióse ágilmente, como posicionándose mejor en el antro donde ignoro cuando habíase refugiado; y, presa de una inquietud verdaderamente propia de un gorila enjaulado, ante las gentes que lo observan y lo asedian, saltaba, gruñía, rascaba en la torta y en el estucado del granero vacío, sin descuidarse de mí ni por un solo momento, presto a la defensa y al ataque.

—¡Padre mío!—rompí a suplicarle, impotente y débil para lanzarme a sus brazos.

Mi padre entonces depuso bruscamente su aire diabólico, desarmó toda su traza indómita y pareció salvar de un solo impulso toda la noche de su pensamiento. Deslizóse en seguida hacia mí, manso, suave, tierno, dulce, transfigurado, hombre, como debió de acercarse a mi madre el día en que se estrecharon tanto y tan humanamente, hasta sacar la sangre con que llenaron mi corazón y lo impulsaron a latir a compás de mis sienes y mis plantas.

Pero cuando yo ya creía haber hecho la luz en él, al conjuro milagroso del clamor filial, se detuvo a pocos pasos de mí, como enmendándose allá, en el misterio de su mente enferma. La expresión de su faz barbada y enflaquecida fue entonces tan desorbitada y lejana, y, sin embargo, tan fuerte y de tanta vida interior, que me crispó hasta hacerme doblar la mirada, envolviéndome en una sensación de frío y de completo trastorno de la realidad.

Volví, no obstante, a hablarle con toda vehemencia. Sonrió extrañamente.

—La estrella . . .—balbuceó con sorda fatiga. Y otra vez lanzó agrios chillidos.

La angustia y el terror me hicieron sudar glacialmente. Exhalé un medroso sollozo, rodé la escalinata sin sentido y salí de la casa.

La noche había caído del todo.

¡Es que mi padre estaba loco! ¡Es que también él y todos los míos creíanse cuadrumanos, del mismo modo que la familia de Urquizo! Mi casa habíase convertido, pues, en un manicomio. ¡El contagio de los parientes! ¡Sí; la influencia fatal!

Pero esto no era todo. Una cosa más atroz y asoladora había acontecido. Un flagelo del destino; una ira de Dios. No sólo en mi hogar estaban locos. Lo estaba el pueblo entero y todos sus alrededores.

Una vez fuera de la casa, echéme a caminar sin saber adónde ni con qué fin, padeciendo aquí y allá choques y cataclismos morales tan hondos que antes ni después los ha habido semejantes que abatieran más mi sensibilidad.

Las calles tenían aspecto de tapiados caminos. Por doquiera que salíame al paso algún transeúnte, saltaba en él fatalmente una simulación de antropoide, un personaje mímico. La obsesión zoológica regresiva, cuyo germen primero brotara tantos años ha en la testa funámbula de Luis Urquizo, hablase propagado en todos y cada uno de los habitantes de Cayna, sin variar absolutamente de naturaleza. A todos aquellos infelices les había dado por la misma idea. Todos habían sido mordidos en la misma curva cerebral.

No conservo recuerdo de una noche más preñada de tragedia y bestialidad, en cuyo fondo de cortantes bordes no había más luz que la natural de los astros, ya que en ninguna parte alcancé a ver luz artificial. ¡Hasta el fuego, obra y signo fundamentales de humanidad, había sido proscrito de allí! Como a través de los dominios de una todavía ignorada especie animal de transición, peregriné por ese lamentable caos donde no pude dar, por mucho que lo quise y lo busqué, con persona alguna que librado hubiérase de él. Por lo visto, había desaparecido de allí todo indicio de civilidad.

Muy poco tiempo después de mi salida, debí de haber tornado a mi casa. Advertíme de pronto en el primer corredor. Ni un ruido. Ni un aliento. Corté la compacta oscuridad que reinaba, crucé el extenso patio y di con el corredor de enfrente. ¿Qué sería de mi padre y de toda mi familia?

Alguna serenidad tocó mi ánima transida. Había que buscar a todo trance y sin pérdida de tiempo a mi madre, y verla y saberla sana y salva y acariciarla y oírla que llora de ternura y que gozo al reconocerme, y rehacer, a su presencia, todo el hogar deshecho. Había que buscar de nuevo a mi padre. Quizás, por otro lado, sólo él estaría enfermo. Quizás todos los demás gozarían del pleno ejercicio de sus facultades mentales.

¡Oh, sí, Dios mío! Engañado habíame, sin duda, al generalizar de tan ligero modo. Ahora caía en cuenta de mi nerviosidad del primer momento y de lo mal dispuesta que había estado mi excitable fantasía para haber levantado tan horribles castillos en el aire. Y aun ¿acaso podía estar seguro de la demencia misma de mi padre?

Una fresca brisa de esperanza acaricióme hasta las entrañas.

Franqueé, disparado de alegría, la primera puerta que alcancé entre la oscuridad, y, al avanzar hacia adentro, sin saber por qué, sentí que vacilaba, al mismo tiempo que, inconscientemente, extraía de uno de los bolsillos una caja de fósforos y prendía fuego.

Escudriñaba la habitación, cuando oí unos pasos que se aproximaban por los corredores. Parecían atropellarse.

La sangre desapareció del todo de mi cuerpo; pero no tanto que ello me obligase a abandonar la cerilla que acababa de encender.

Mi padre, tal como le había visto aquella tarde, apareció en el umbral de la puerta, seguido de algunos seres siniestros que chillaban grotescamente. Apagaron de un revuelo la luz que yo portaba, ululando con fatídico misterio:

—¡Luz! ¡Luz! ... ¡Una estrella!

Yo me quedé helado y sin palabra.

Más, de modo intempestivo, cobré luego todas mis fuerzas para clamar desesperado:

—¡Padre mío! ¡Recuerda que soy tu hijo! ¡Tú no estás enfermo! ¡Tú no puedes estar enfermo! ¡Deja ese gruñido de las selvas! ¡Tú no eres un mono! ¡Tú eres un hombre, oh, padre mío! ¡Todos nosotros somos hombres!

E hice lumbre de nuevo.

Una carcajada vino a apuñalarme de sesgo a sesgo el corazón. Y mi padre gimió con desgarradora lástima, lleno de piedad infinita.

—¡Pobre! Se cree hombre. Está loco....

La oscuridad se hizo otra vez.

Y arrebatado por el espanto, me alejé de aquel grupo tenebroso, la cabeza tambaleante.

—¡Pobre! — exclamaron todos — ¡Está completamente loco!...

❖ —Y aquí me tienen ustedes, loco —agregó tristemente el hombre que nos había hecho tan extraña narración.

Acercósele en esto un empleado, uniformado de amarillo y de indolencia, y le indicó que le siguiera, al mismo tiempo que nos saludaba, despidiéndose de soslayo:

—Buenas tardes. Le llevo ya a su celda. Buenas tardes.

Y el loco narrador de aquella historia, perdióse lomo a lomo con su enfermero que le guiaba por entre los verdes chopos del asilo; mientras el mar lloraba amargamente y peleaban dos pájaros en el hombro jadeante de la tarde....

MIRTHO

Orate de candor, aposéntome bajo la uña índiga del firmamento y en las 9 uñas restantes de mis manos, sumo, envuelvo y arramblo los dígitos fundamentales, de 1 en fondo, hacia la más alta conciencia de las derechas.

Orate de amor, con qué ardentía la amo.

Yo la encontré, al viento el velo lila, que iba diciendo a las tiernas lascas de sus sienes: "Hermanitas, no se atrasen, no se atrasen...." Alfaban sus senos, dragoneando por la ciudad de barro, con estridor de mandatos y amenazas. Quebróse, ¡ay! en la esquina el impávido cuerpo: yo sufrí en todas mis puntas, ante tamaño heroísmo de belleza, ante la inminencia de ver humear sangre estética, ante la muerte mártir de la euritmia de esa carnatura viva, ante la posible falla de un lombar que resiste o de una nervadura rebelde que de pronto se apeala y cede a la contraria. ¡Mas he allí la espartana victoria de ese escorzo! Y cuánta sabiduría, en metalla caliente, cernía la forja de aquese desfiladero de nervios, por todas las pasmadas bocas de mi alma. Y luego, sus muslos y sus piernas y sus prisioneros pies. Y sobre todo, su vientre.

Sí. Su vientre, más atrevido que la frente misma; más palpitante que el corazón, corazón él mismo. Cetrería de halconados futuros de aquilinos parpadeos sobre la sombra del misterio. ¡Quién más que él! Adorado criadero de eternidad, tubulado de todas las corrientes historiadas y venideras del pensamiento y del amor. Vientre portado sobre el arco vaginal de toda felicidad, y en el intercolumnio mismo de las dos piernas, de la vida y la muerte, de la noche y el día, del ser y el no ser. Oh vientre de la mujer, donde Dios tiene su único hipogeo inescrutable, su sola tienda terrenal en que se abriga cuando baja, cuando sube al país del dolor, del placer y de las lágrimas. ¡A Dios sólo se le puede hallar en el vientre de la mujer!

❖ Tales cosas decía ayer tarde un joven amigo mío, mientras con él discurríamos por el jirón de la Unión. Yo me reía a carcajada limpia. Es claro. El pobre está enamorado de una de tantas bellas mujeres que cruzan por la arteria principal de Lima, elegantes y distinguidas, de 5 a 7 de la tarde. Ayer el ocaso ardía urente de verano. Sol, lujo, flirt, encanto sensual por todas partes. Y mi amigo desflagraba romántico y apasionado, hecho un poseído de veras. Sí. Hecho un orate de amor, como él llamábase entre orgulloso y combatido. Un orate de amor.

Despedíme de él, y, ya a solas, llegué a decirme para mí: Orate de amor. Bueno. Pero ¿qué quería significar aquello de orate de candor, apóstrofe de ironía con que inició su jerigonza?

Anoche vino a mí el mozo.

—Escúcheme usted—me dijo, sentándose a mi lado y encendiendo un cigarrillo—. Escúcheme cuanto voy a referirle ahora mismo, ya que ello es harto extraordinario, para quedar oculto para siempre.

Miróme con melancolía que taladraba y, echando luego temerosas y repetidas ojeadas hacia los ventanales del aposento, con sigilo y gravedad profunda continuó de este modo:

—¿Usted conoce a la mujer que amo?

—No—le repliqué al punto.

—Perfectamente. No la conoce. Pues ríase de cómo la esbocé esta tarde. Nada. Esas frases eran sólo truncos neoramas de la gran equis encantada que es la existencia de tan peregrina criatura.

Y armando cinegético, disparado ceño de quien fuera a capturar las invisibles alimañas, saltó los ojos quizás a un metro fuera de las órbitas, hizo rechinar los dientes y hasta las encías contra las encías, flagelóse desde los lóbulos de las orejas desoladas hasta la punta de la nariz con un relámpago morado; clavó frenético ambas manos entre la greña de erizo como para mesársela, y deletreó con voz de visionario que casi me hace estallar en risotadas:

—Mi amada es 2.

—Sigue usted incomprensible. ¿Su amada es 2? ¿Qué quiere decir eso? Mi amigo sacudió la cabeza abatiéndose.

—Mirtho, la amada mía, es 2. Usted sonríe. Está bien. Pero ya verá la verdad de esta aseveración.

—A Mirtho—agregó—la conocí hace cinco meses en Trujillo, entre una adorable farándula de muchachas y muchachos compañeros míos de bohemia. Mirtho pulsaba a la sazón catorce setiembre tónicos, una cinta milagrosa de sangre virginal y primavera. La adoro desde entonces. Hasta aquí lo corriente y racional. Mas he allí que, poco tiempo después, el más amado e inteligente de mis amigos díjome de buenas a primeras: "¿Por qué es usted tan malo con Mirtho? ¿Por qué, sabiendo cuánto le ama, la deja usted a menudo para cortejar a otra mujer? No sea así nunca con esa pobre chica."

Tan inesperada como infundada acusación, en vez de suscitar mi protesta e inducirme a reiterar mi fidelidad a Mirtho, toméla, como comprenderá usted, solo en son de inocente y alado calembour de amistad y nada más, y sonreí para pasmo de mi amigo que, dada su austera y purísima moral en materia de amor, tuvo entonces un suave mohín de reproche hacia mí, arguyéndome que cuanto acababa de decirme tenía toda seriedad. Y, sin embargo, yo nunca había estado con mujer alguna que no fuese Mirtho desde que la conocí. Absolutamente. La queja de mi amigo carecía, pues, de base de realidad; y, si ella no hubiera venido de un espíritu tan fraternal como aquél, habríame dejado sin duda tranquilo y exento del escozor en la conciencia. Pero el cariño casi paternal con que trataba aquel amigo inolvidable todos los acontecimientos de mi vida, investía a tan extraño reproche de un toque asaz inquietante y digno de atención, para que él no me lastimase sin saber por qué. Además por el gran amor que yo sentía hacia Mirtho, dolíame que aquello viniese a perturbar así nuestra dicha.

Desde entonces, continuamente aquel amigo repetíame el consabido reproche, cada vez con más acritud. Yo, a mi vez, reiterábale y pretendía patentizarle por todos los medios posibles mi lealtad para Mirtho. Vanos esfuerzos. Nada. La acusación marchaba, afirmándose con tal terquedad que empezaba yo a creer a su autor fuera de razón, cuando llegó momento en que todos los demás hermanos de bohemia fueron de uno en uno formulándome idéntica tacha a mi conducta.

—Nosotros, todo el mundo—recriminábanme desaforadamente—te hemos sorprendido infraganti, y con nuestros propios ojos. Nada tienes que alegar en contrario. Tú no puedes negar la verdad.

Y en efecto. Si a cuantos me conocían hubiera yo interrogado sobre la verdad de este asunto, todos habrían testificado mis relaciones de amor con la segunda mujer para mí tan desconocida como irreal. Y yo habríame quedado aún más boquiabierto ante semejante fosfeno colectivo, que no otra cosa podía acontecer en el cerebro de mis acusadores.

Pero una circunstancia llamaba mi atención, y era que Mirtho nunca me decía nada que diera a entender ni remotamente que ella supiese de mi supuesta infidelidad. Ni un gesto, ni una espina en su alma, no obstante su carácter vehemente y celoso. De la ciudad entera ¿acaso sólo ella ignoraba mi culpa y ni presentía a través de las generales murmuraciones? Muy más, si, como me lo echaban en cara, diz que yo solía presentarme por doquiera y sin escrúpulo alguno con la otra. Por todo esto, la ignorancia de parte de Mirtho roíame el corazón al otro lado de la acusación de los demás. En aquella ignorancia, podría asegurar, radicaba de misteriosa manera y por inextricable encadenamiento de motivos, la piedra de toque, y quizás hasta la razón de ser de la imputación que se me hacía.

Mirtho, sin duda alguna, no sabía, pues, nada de la otra. Esto era incuestionable. Malhadada inocencia suya, en último examen, porque ella, no sé por qué medios, vino a dar a la habladuría azotante de los demás, una cierta vida, un calor y ¡vamos! un sabor de intriga tales, que yo no podía menos que sentirme vacilar arrastrado hasta el filo de una ridícula posición de desconcierto y de absurda atonía.

Ocasión llegó en que habiendo asistido en unión de Mirtho al teatro, nos hallábamos ambos juntos en la sala, cuando en uno de los entreactos, dieron mis ojos con uno de mis amigos. Este distinguióme a su vez e hízome señas para que saliese a atenderle al foyer. Harto nos amábamos con ese muchacho para que, por inusitada que fuera tal invitación en ese instante, yo no la atendiese. Pedí perdón a Mirtho y salí a verle.

—¡Ahora no lo negarás!—exclamó aquel amigo desde lejos—. Allí estás ahora mismo con la otra.... ¡Y cuánto se parece a Mirtho!

Repliquéle que no, que él no se había fijado. Fue todo inútil.

Despedíme riendo y volví al lado de Mirtho, sin haber dado mayor importancia a lo que creí un simple juego de camarada y nada más.

Varias veces, posteriormente, estando con ella, tuve, no sin fuertes sobresaltos y alarmas que terminaban es cierto en seguida, repentina impresión de hallarme en efecto ante otra mujer que no era Mirtho. Hubo noche, por ejemplo, en que esta crisis de duda colmóse en álgida desesperación, por haber percibido un inusitado arrebol de serenidad en el desenvolvimiento de las ondas de un silencio suyo, arrebol completamente extraño a todas las pausas de su voz, y que chilló aquella noche en todo mi corazón. Pero, repito, esas alarmas cedían luego, pensando que ellas deberíanse sin duda a la sugestión obsesiva que podían ejercer los demás cerca de mí.

He de advertir, por lo que esto pudiera dar luz a este enredo, que por raro que parezca el caso, fuera de la vez en que fui presentado a Mirtho, jamás la vi acompañada de tercera persona, y aun más: cuando solía hallarse conmigo, nunca estuvimos sino los dos únicamente.

Así continuaban las cosas, creciente pesadilla que iba a volverme loco, hasta cierta mañana tibia y diáfana en que hallábame en la confitería Marrón, tomando algunos refrescos en compañía de Mirtho. Ante la parva mesa de albo caucho traslúcido estábamos a solas.

—Oye—la murmuré lacerado, como quien manotea a ciegas en un precipicio, mientras las flotantes manos suyas, de un cárdeno espasmódico, subieron a asentar el cabello en sus sienes invisibles—¿Quieres decirme una cosa?

Ella sonrió llena de ternura y acaso con cierto frenesí.

—¡Oye, Mirtho adorada!—repetíla titubeante.

Interrumpióme violentamente y me clavó sus ojos de hembra en celo, arguyéndome:

—¿Qué dices? ¿Mirtho? ¿Estás loco? ¿Con cara de quién me ves?

Y luego, sin dejarme aducir palabra:

—¿Qué Mirtho es esa? ¡Ah! Con que me eres infiel y amas a otra. Amas a otra mujer que se llama Mirtho.

¡Qué tal! ¡Así pagas mi amor! Y sollozó inconsolable.

❖ Calló el adolescente relator. Y, al difuso fulgor de la pantalla, parecióme ver animarse a ambos lados del agitado mozo, dos idénticas formas fugitivas, elevarse suavemente por sobre la cabeza del amante, y luego confundirse en el alto ventanal, y alejarse y deshacerse entre un rehilo telescópico de pestañas.

CERA

Aquella noche no pudimos fumar. Todos los ginkés de Lima estaban cerrados. Mi amigo, que conducíame por entre los taciturnos dédalos de la conocida mansión amarilla de la calle Hoyos, donde se dan numerosos fumaderos, despidióse por fin de mí, y aporcelanadas alma y pituitarias, asaltó el primer eléctrico urbano y esfumóse entre la madrugada.

Todavía me sentía un tanto ebrio de los últimos alcoholes. ¡Oh mi bohemia de entonces, broncería esquinada siempre de balances impares, enconchada de secos paladares, el círculo de mi cara libertad de hombre a dos aceras de realidad hasta por tres sienes de imposible! Pero perdonadme estos desahogos que tienen aún bélico olor a perdigones fundidos en arrugas.

Digo que sentíame todavía ebrio cuando vime ya solo, caminando sin rumbo por los barrios asiáticos de la ciudad. Mucho a mucho aclarábase mi espíritu. Luego hice la cuenta de lo que me sucedía. Una inquietud posó en mi izquierdo pezón. Berbiquí hecho de una hebra de la cabellera negra y brillante de mi novia perdida para siempre, la inquietud picó, revoloteó, se prolongó hacia adentro y traspasóme en todas direcciones. Entonces no habría podido dormir. Imposible. Sufría el redolor de mi felicidad trunca, cuyos destellos trabajados ahora en férrea tristeza irremediable, asomaban larvados en los más hondos paréntesis de mi alma, como a decirme con misteriosa ironía, que mañana, que sí, que como no, que otra vez, que bueno.

Quise entonces fumar. Necesitaba yo alivio para mi crisis nerviosa. Encaminéme al ginké de Chale, que estaba cerca.

Con la cautela del caso llegué a la puerta. Paré el oído. Nada. Después de breve espera, dispúseme a retirarme de allí, cuando oí que alguien saltaba de la tarima y caminaba descalzo y precipitadamente dentro de la habitación. Traté de aguaitar, a fin de saber si había allí algún camarada. Por la cerradura de la puerta alcancé a distinguir que Chale hacía luz, y sentábase con gran desplazamiento de malhumor delante de la lamparita de aceite, cuyo verdor patógeno soldóse en mustio semitono a la lámina facial del chino, soflamada de visible iracundia. Nadie más estaba allí.

Dado el aspecto de inexpugnable de Chale, y, según el cual, parecía acabar de despertar de alguna mala pesadilla quizás, consideré importuna mi presencia y resolví marcharme, cuando el asiático abrió uno de los cajones de la mesa y, capitaneando de alguna voz de mando interior e inexorable, que desenvainóle el cuerpo entero en resuelto avance, extrajo de un lacónico estuche de pulimentado cedro, unos cuerpos blancos entre las uñas lancinantes y asquerosas. Los puso en el borde de la mesa. Eran dos trozos de mármol.

La curiosidad tentóme. Dos trozos ¿de mármol eran? Eran de mármol. No sé por qué, desde el primer momento, esas piezas, sin haberlas tocado ni visto claramente y de cerca, vinieron a través del espacio, a barajarse entre las yemas de mis dedos, produciéndome la más segura y cierta sensación del mármol.

El chino las volvió a coger, angulando en el aire miradas por demás febriles y de angustioso devaneo, para que ellas no descorrieran ante mí ciertas presunciones sobre la causa de su vigilia. Las cogió y examinólas detenidamente a la luz. Sí. Dos pedazos de mármol.

Luego, sin abandonarlos, acodado en la mesa, desaguó entre dientes algún monosílabo canalla que alcanzó apenas a ensartarse en el ojo tajado, donde el alma del chino lagrimeó de ambición mezclada de impotencia. Hala otra vez el mismo cajón y aupado acaso por un viejo tesón que redivivía por centésima vez, toma de allí numerosos aceros, y con ellos empieza a labrar sus mármoles de cábala.

Ciertas presunciones, dije antes, saltaron ante mí. En efecto. Conocía yo desde dos años atrás a Chale. El mongol era jugador. Y jugador de fama en Lima; perdedor de millares, ganador de tesoros al decir de las gentes. ¿Qué podía significar, pues, entonces esa vela tormentosa, ese episodio furibundo de artífice nocturno? ¿Y esos dos fragmentos de piedra? Y luego, ¿por qué dos y no uno, tres o más? ¡Eureka! ¡Dos dados! Dos dados en gestación.

El chino labraba, labraba desde el vértice mismo de la noche. Su faz, entre tanto, también labraba una infinita sucesión de líneas. Momentos hubo que Chale exaltábase y quería romper aquellos cuerpezuelos que irían a correr sobre el tapete persiguiéndose entre sí, a las ganadas del azar y la suerte, con el ruido de dos cerrados puños de una misma persona, que se diesen duro el uno al otro, hasta hacer chispas.

Por mi parte habíame interesado tanto esa escena, que no pensé ni por mucho abandonarla. Parecía tratarse de una vieja empresa de paciente y heroico desarrollo. Y yo aguzábame la mente, indagando lo que perseguiría este enfermo de destino. Burilar un par de dados. ¿Y bien?

Tanto se afirma sobre maniobras digitales y secretas desviaciones o enmiendas a voluntad en el cubileteo del juego, que, sin duda, díjeme al cabo, algo de esto se propone mi hombre. Esto por lo que tocaba al fin. Pero lo que más me intrigaba, como se comprenderá, era el arte de los medios, en cuya disposición parecía empeñarse Chale a la sazón, esto es la correlación que debía de preestablecerse, entre la clase de dados y las posibilidades dinámicas de las manos. Porque si no fuese necesaria esta concurrencia bilateral de elementos, ¿para qué este chino hacía por sí mismo, los dados? Pues cualquier material rodante sería utilizable para el caso. Pero no.

Es indudable que los dados deben de estar hechos de cierta materia, bajo este peso, con aquel aristaje, exagonados sobre tal o cual impalpable declive para ser despedidos por las yemas de los dedos; y luego, estar pulidos con esa otra depresión o casi inmaterial aspereza entre marca y marca de los puntos o entre un ángulo poliédrico y el exergo en blanco de una de las cuatro caras correspondientes. Hay, pues, que suscitar la aptitud de la materia aleatoria, para hacer posible su obediencia y docilidad a las vibraciones humanas, en este punto siempre improvisadas, y triunfadoras por eso, de la mano, que piensa y calcula aún en la más oscuro y ciego de estos avatares.

Y si no, había que observar al asiático en su procelosa jornada creadora, cincel en mano, picando, rayando, partiendo, desmoronando, hurgando las condiciones de armonía y dentaje entre las innacidas proporciones del dado y las propias ignoradas potencias de su voluntad cambiante. A veces, detenía su labor un punto, contemplaba el mármol y sonreía su rostro de vicioso, melado por la lumbre de la lámpara. Luego con aire tranquilo y amplio, golpeaba, cambiaba de acero, hacía rodar el juguete monstruoso ensayándolo, confrontaba planos tenaz, pacientemente y cavilaba.

Pocas semanas después de aquella noche, quienes hubo que murmuraban entre atorrantes y demás círculos de la cuerda, cosas estupefacientes e increíbles sobre grandes acontecimientos recientemente habidos en las casas de juego de Lima. De mañana en mañana las leyendas fabulosas crecían. Una tarde del último invierno, en la puerta del Palais Concert, refería un exótico personaje de biscotelas chorreantes, a un grupo de mozos, que le oían por todas las orejas:

—Chale para poder jugar esos diez mil soles, no ha jugado limpio. Yo no sé cómo. Pero el chino se maneja una misteriosa, inconstatable prestidigitación sobre el tapete. Eso no se puede negar. Fíjense ustedes— recalcó aquel hombre con gravedad siniestra—que los dados con que juega ese chino, jamás aparecen en la mano de otro jugador que no sea Chale. Hablo sobre datos inequívocos de propia observación. Esos dados tienen, pues, algo. En fin . . . Yo no sé. . . .

Una noche lanzóme la inquietud al antro donde jugaba Chale.

Era una cosa de juego para los más soberbios duelos del tapete.

Había mucha gente en torno de la mesa. La cabestreada atención de todos hacia el paño ganglionado de montones de billetes, díjome que esa era noche de gran borrasca. Abriéronme paso algunos conocidos que entusiastas me echaban a apostar.

Allí estaba Chale. Desde la cabecera de la mesa, presidía la sesión, en su impasible y torturante catadura todopoderosa: dos correas verticales por cuello, desde los parietales chatos de ralo pelaje, hasta las barras lívidas de las clavículas; boca forjada a la mala en dos jebes tensos de codicia, que no se entreabrían jamás en sonrisa por miedo a desnudarse hasta el hueso; camisa heroica hasta los codos. El latido de la vida saltábale de un pulso al otro, buscando las puertas de las manos para escapar de cuerpo tan miserable. Livor nauseante sobre los pómulos de caza.

Podría decirse que allí se había perdido la facultad de hablar. Señas. Adverbios casi inarticulados. Interjecciones arrastradas. ¡Oh cuánto quema a veces el resuello branquial de lo que anda muerto, y sin embargo vivo en cada uno de nosotros!

Propúseme observar con toda la sutileza y profundidad de que era capaz, las más mínimas ondas sicológicas y mecánicas del chino.

Rayaba la una de la madrugada.

Alguien apostó cinco mil soles a la suerte. El aire chasqueó como agua caliente estocada por la primera burbuja de la ebullición. Y si quisiera yo ahora precisar cómo eran las caras circunstantes en aquellos segundos de prueba, diría que todas ellas rebasáronse a sí mismas y fueron a ser refregadas y estrujadas con el par de dados de Chale, encendiéndose y afilándose allí, hasta urgir y querer arrancar una novena arista milagrosa a cada dado, como ansiada sonrisa del destino. Chale deshízose violentamente de los dados, como un par de brasas que chisporroteasen, y rugió una hienada formidable grosería que trascendió en la sala a carne muerta.

Palpéme en mi propio cuerpo como buscándome, y me di cuenta de que allí estaba yo temblando de asombro. ¿Qué había sentido el chino? ¿Por qué arrojó los dados así, como si le hubiesen quemado o cortado las manos? ¿El ánimo de aquellos jugadores todos, como es natural, en contra suya siempre, había, ante tan crestada apuesta, así llegádole a herir de tal manera?

Mientras los dados estuviesen abandonados sobre el paño de esmeralda, vinieron a mi memoria los dos trozos de mármol que vi troquelar a Chale en ya lejana noche. Estos dados, que ahora veía, provenían por cierto de las nacientes joyas de entonces, porque he aquí que ellos eran de un mármol albicante y traslúcido en los bordes y de brillo firme casi metálico en los fondos. ¡Bellos cubos de Dios!

El chino, luego de corta vacilación, recogió otra vez los dados y siguió su juego, no sin algún temblor convaleciente en las sienes que quizás sólo yo percibí con harto trabajo.

Tiró una vez. Barajó. Volvió a tirar dos, tres, cuatro, cinco, seis, siete, ocho veces. La novena pintó quina y sena.

Todos parecieron descolgarse de una picota y resucitar. Todos humanizáronse de nuevo. Por allí se pidió un cigarrillo. Tosieron. Chale pagó dos mil quinientos soles. Yo lancé un suspiro. Luego tragué saliva. Hacía calor.

Formuláronse nuevas apuestas y continuó la trágica disputa de la suerte con la suerte.

Noté que la pérdida que acababa de tener Chale no le había inmutado absolutamente, circunstancia que venía a echar aún mayor sombra de misterio sobre el motivo de su inusitado rapto de ira anterior que, por lo visto, no podía atribuirse a claro alguno producido fogonazo nervioso, por incausado, al parecer, socavaba mi espíritu con crecientes cavilaciones sobre posibles inteligencias del chino con corrientes o potencias que danse más allá de los hechos y de la realidad perceptible. ¿Hasta dónde, en efecto, podría Chale parcializar al destino en su favor por medio de una técnica sabia e infalible en el manejo de los dados?

En el primer juego que siguió al de los cinco mil soles, fue de nuevo esta misma cantidad, apuntada esta vez al azar. Varios acompañaron con menores apuestas a las quinientas libras. Y el ambiente de combate fuéle ahora aún más enteramente hostil al banquero.

Los dados saltaron de la diestra del asiático, juntos, al mismo tiempo, dotados de un impulso igual. Con un instrumento de medida que pudiese registrar en cifras innominables las humanas ecuaciones gestadoras de acción más infinitesimales, habríase constatado la simultaneidad absolutamente matemática con que ambos mármoles fueron despedidos al espacio. Y juraría que, al auscultar la relación de avance que desarrollábase entre esos dos dados al iniciar su vuelo, lo que hay de más permanente, de más vivo, de más fuerte, de más inmutable y eterno en mi ser, fundidas todas las potencias de la dimensión física, se dio contra sí mismo, y así pude sentir entonces en la verdad del espíritu, la partida material de esos dos vuelos, a un mismo tiempo, unánimes.

Chale había arrojado los dados constriñendo toda su escultura hacia una desviación anatómica tan rara y singular, que ello turbó aún más mi ya sugestionada sensibilidad. Diríase que en ese momento había el jugador estilizado toda su animalidad, subordinándola a un pensamiento y un deseo únicos a la sazón en su juego.

En efecto. ¿Cómo poder describir semejante movimiento de sus huesosos flancos, arrimándose uno contra otro, por sobre la gritería misma de un silencio de pie suspenso entre los dos guijarros de la marcha; semejante ritmo de los omóplatos transfigurándose, empollándose en truncas alas que, de pronto, crecían y salían fuera, ante la ceguedad de todos los jugadores que nada de esto percibían y que me dejaban ¡ay, sólo ante aquel espectáculo que me castigaba en todo el corazón! . . . Y aquella confluencia del hombro derecho, quieta, esperando que la frente del chino acabase de ganar todo el arco que la intuición y el cálculo mental de fuerzas, distancias, obstáculos, elementos aceleratrices y hasta del máximum de intervención de una segunda potestad humana, tendían, templaban, ajustaban desde el punto más alto de la vidente voluntad del hombre hasta los cercos lindantes a la omnipotencia divina. . . . Y esa muñeca pálida, alambreada, neurótica, como de hechicería, casi diafanizada por la luz que parecía portar y transmitir en vértigo a los dados, que la esperaban en la cuenca de la mano, saltando, hidrogénicos, palpitantes, cálidos, blandos, sumisos, transustanciados tal vez, en dos trozos de cera que sólo detendríanse en el punto del extendido paño, secretamente requerido, plasmados por los dos lados que plugo al jugador. . . .

La presencia entera de Chale y toda la atmósfera de extraordinaria e ineludible soberanía que desarrolló en la sala en tal instante, habíanme envuelto también a mí, como átomo en medio del fuego solar del mediodía.

Los dados volaron, mejor, corrieron tropezándose entre sí, patinando, saltando isócronos a veces, con el rehilo punzante de dos tambores que batieran en redoble de piedra la marcha de lo que no podía volver atrás, aun a pesar de Dios mismo, ante las pobres miradas de aquella estancia, solemne y recogida más que iglesia a la hora de alzar la hostia consagrada....

Vibrante, grisácea línea trababa cada dado al rodar. Una de esas líneas empezó a engrosar, fue desdoblándose en manchas unas más blancas que otras; pintó sucesivamente 2 puntos negros, luego 5, 4, 2, 3 y plantóse por fin marcando quina. El otro mármol ¡oh los costados y el espaldar, el hombre y el frontal del jugador! el otro mármol ¡oh la partida simultánea de los dados! el otro avanzó tres dedos más que el anterior, y por parecido proceso de evolución hacia la meta insospechada, fue a presentar también 5 puntos de carbón sobre el tapete. ¡Suerte!

El chino, con la serenidad de quien lee un enigma cuyos términos le fuesen desde mucho antes familiares, hizo ingresar a su banca los cinco mil soles de la apuesta.

Alguien dijo a media voz:

—¡Es una barbaridad! Siempre las más altas paradas son para Chale. No se puede con él.

El chino, repetí para mí, no hay duda, tiene completo dominio sobre los dados que él mismo labrara, y, acaso, todavía más, es dueño y señor de los más indescifrables designios del destino, que le obedecen ciegamente.

Los más poderosos jugadores parecieron encolerizarse y refunfuñar contra Chale, a raíz de la última jugada. La sala entera sacudióse en un espasmo de despecho; y quizá la protesta amordazada de esa masa de seres a los que así golpeaba la invencible sombra del destino encarnada en la fascinante figura de Chale, estuvo a punto de traducirse en un zarpazo de sangre. Un solo gran infortunio puede más que millares de pequeños triunfos dispersos y los atrae y ata a sus huracanadas entrañas, hasta untarles por fin en su aceite incandescente y funerario. Todos esos hombres debieron sentirse heridos por la última victoria del chino, y, llegado el caso, todos le habrían arrancado la vida a las ganadas. Hasta yo mismo—

me aguijonea el remordimiento al recordarlo—hasta yo mismo odié furiosamente a Chale en ese instante.

Siguió una apuesta de diez mil soles al azar. Todos temblamos de expectación, de miedo y de una misericordia infinita, como si fuésemos a presenciar un heroísmo. La tragedia revolcóse cosquillante a lo largo de las epidermis. Las pupilas relincharon casi vertiendo lloro puro. Los rostros alisáronse cárdenos de incertidumbre. Chale lanzó sus dados. Y de este solo cordelazo, apuntaron dos senas en el paño. ¡Suerte!

Sentí que alguien se abría paso a mi lado y me apartaba para adelantarse a la mesa, presionándome, casi acogotándome en forma brutal y arrolladora, como si una fuerza irresistible y fatal impulsara al intruso para tal conducta. Quienes estuvieron a mi lado sufrieron idéntico vejamen del desconocido.

Y he aquí que le chino, en vez de recoger dinero ganado, hizo de él desusado olvido, para como movido por resorte, volver inmediatamente la cara hacia el nuevo concurrente. Chale se demudó. Parece que ambos hombres chocaron sus miradas, a modo de dos picos que se prueban en el aire.

El recién llegado era un hombre alto y de anchura proporcionada y hasta armoniosa; aire enhiesto; gran cráneo sobre la herradura fornida de un maxilar inferior que reposaba recogido y armado de excesiva dentadura para mascar cabezas y troncos enteros; el declive de los carrillos anchábase de arriba abajo. Ojos mínimos, muy metidos, como si reculasen para luego acometer en insospechadas embestidas, las niñas sin color, produciendo la impresión de dos cuencas vacías. Tostado cutis; cabello bravo; nariz corva y zahareña; frente tempestuosa. Tipo de pelea y aventura, sorpresivo, preñado de sugerencias embrujadas como boas. Hombre inquietante, mortificante a pesar de su alguna belleza; céntrico. ¿Su raza? No acusaba ninguna. Aquella humanidad peregrina quizá carecía de patria étnica.

Tenía innegable traza mundana y hasta de clubman intachable, con su correcto vestir y su distinción, y el desenfado inquirido de sus ademanes.

Apenas este personaje tomó una posición junto al tapete, todo el gas envenenado de ebriedad y codicia, que respirábamos en la sala, inclusive el de la última jugada de diez mil soles, la mayor de la noche, despejóse y desapareció súbitamente. ¿Qué oculto oxígeno traía, pues, aquel hombre? De haberse podido ver el aire entonces, lo habríamos hallado azul, serena y apaciblemente azul. De golpe recobré mi normalidad y la luz de mi conciencia, entre un hálito fresco de renovación sanguínea y de desahogo. Sentí que me liberaba de algo. Hubo un dulce remanso en la expresión de todos los semblantes. El señorío de Chale y todas sus posturas de sortilegio se acabaron.

En cambio, una cosa allí nacía. Una cosa en forma de sensación de curiosidad primero, luego de extrañeza y de espinosa inquietud. Y esa inquietud partía, indudablemente, de la presentación del nuevo parroquiano. Sí. Pues él—yo lo hubiera afirmado con mi cuello—traía algún propósito apabullante, algún designio misterioso.

El asiático estaba demudado. Desde que éste advirtió al desconocido, no volvió a mirarle cara a cara. Por nada. Aseguraría que la tomó miedo y que en él más que en ningún otro de los presentes, el efecto repulsivo y aborrecible que despertaba ese hombre, fue mucho mayor para ser disimulado. Chale le odiaba, le temía. Esa es la palabra: le tenía miedo. Además, nadie había visto jamás a tal caballero en aquella casa de juego. Chale ni siquiera le conocía. Detonaba, pues, también por esto su presencia.

El clubman de súbito empezó a respirar con trabajo, como si se asfixiara. Jadeaba mirando fijamente al cabizbajo chino que parecía triturado por aquella mirada, mutilado, reducida a pobres carbones toda su personalidad moral, toda su confianza en sí mismo de antes, toda su beligerancia triunfadora siempre del hado. Chale, cariacontecido, como niño cogido en falta, movía los dedos en el hueco de su diestra temblorosa, queriendo derribarlos por impotencia.

El corro, poco a poco, llegó a converger todas sus miradas en el forastero que aún no había pronunciado palabra. Se hizo silencio.

Por fin el recién llegado dijo dirigiéndose al chino:

—¿Cuánto importa toda su banca?

El interrogado pestañeó haciendo una mueca apocalíptica y ridícula de desamparo, como si fuese a recibir una bofetada mortal. Y volviendo en sí, balbuceó, sin saber lo que decía.

—Allí está todo.

La banca importaba más o menos cincuenta mil soles.

El hombre equis nombró esta suma, extrajo una cantidad igual de su cartera y con majestad la colocó en el paño, apostándola al azar, ante el pasmo de los circunstantes. El chino se mordió los labios. Y, siempre rehuyendo el rostro de su nuevo adversario, empezó a barajar los cubos de mármol, sus cubos.

Nadie acompañó a tan monstruosa y atrevida apuesta.

El apostador único, solitario, sin que nadie, absolutamente nadie, menos el chino, pudiese advertirlo, extrajo del bolsillo su revólver, acercólo sigilosamente al cerebro de Chale, y, la mano en el gatillo, erecto el cañón hacia aquel blanco. Nadie, repito, percibió esta espada de Damocles que quedó suspendida sobre la vida del asiático. Muy al contrario. La espada de Damocles viéronla todos suspendida sobre la fortuna del desconocido, pues que su pérdida estaba descontada. Recordé lo que momentos antes habíase susurrado en la sala:

—Siempre las más altas paradas son para Chale. No se pude con él.

¿Era su buena suerte? ¿Era su sabiduría? No lo sé. Pero yo era ahora el primero que preveía la victoria del chino.

Echó éste los dados. ¡Oh los costados y el espaldar, el hombro y el frontal del jugador! De nuevo, y con más óptima elocuencia, repitiese ante mis ojos y ante mi alma, el espectáculo extraordinario, la desviación anatómica, la polarización de toda la voluntad que doma y sojuzga, entraba y dirige los más inextricables designios de la fatalidad. De nuevo, ante el esfuerzo creador del lanzador de dados, sobrecogido fui de un cataclismo misterioso que rompía toda armonía y razón de ser de los hechos y leyes y enigmas en mi cerebro estupefacto. De nuevo esa partida simultánea de los dados ante iguales términos aleatorios de apuesta. De nuevo abrí los ojos desmesurándolos para constatar la suerte que vendría a agraciar al gran banquero.

Los mármoles corrieron y corrieron y corrieron.

El cañón y el gatillo y la mano esperaban. El de la gran parada no miraba los dados: sólo miraba fija, terrible, implacablemente a la testa del asiático.

Ante aquel desafío, que nadie notaba, de ese revólver contra ese par de dados que pintarían el número que pluga a la invencible sombra del Destino, encarnada en la figura de Chale, cualquier habría asegurado que yo estaba allí. Pero no. Yo no estaba allí.

Los dados detuviéronse. La muerte y el destino tiraron de todos los pelos.

¡Dos ases!

El chino se echó a llorar como un niño.

3. Néstor Vallejo (*left*) and César Vallejo (*right*), 1920.
Courtesy of Jorge Kishimoto.

Appendix

No biographer or scholar can avoid the imprisonment that César Vallejo suffered between November 6, 1920, and February 12, 1921, in Trujillo, an episode that stakes out an indubitable before and after in the life and work of the Santiaguino. His later exile in Paris has its origin in his prosecution for the events that took place in his hometown of Santiago de Chuco on August 1, 1920, and many poems from *Trilce* and short stories from *Scales* allude to the anguishing situation experienced in prison. Antenor Orrego—friend and member of the celebrated Grupo Norte—testified to the anxiety with which Vallejo endured those circumstances in jail.

Some of the letters that Vallejo wrote in France mention arrest warrants issued by the Trujillo Court, thus confirming that legal proceedings were pending and that Vallejo, in effect, was a fugitive. On February 26, 1928, seven years after his release from prison, a letter written to Carlos Godoy—the attorney who handled the pardon—announced his acquittal: "I've just received news from my family," Vallejo writes, "saying that the Court has finally decreed the prescription of the famous case brought against me and others over the events of August 1920."[1]

In the midst of the brutal events that led to a few deaths and fires in his hometown, Vallejo's implication appears to be distorted when seen in relation to a personal vendetta of the powerful and influential merchant Carlos Santa María, who pushed for the prosecution and trial through all possible means. On the other hand, there is the activity of Vallejo's friends in Grupo Norte and the prestige as a writer that he already had on a local level that helped to achieve the provisional release. These early years are the object of many investigations that try to figure out the labyrinths of the great Peruvian poet.

In October 2014, and in the context of the Congreso Internacional Vallejo Siempre, I had the opportunity to enter the ruins that remain of this emblematic jail—in addition to Vallejo's episode, various historical events of Peru had this prison as a protagonist. The building is located near the main plaza, near the building where Vallejo and his brother Néstor rented a room, and the Universidad de Trujillo, where he earned his bachelor's degree with the thesis "Romanticism in Castilian Poetry."

Despite the advanced deterioration, one can still recognize the structure, with its high walls surrounding the central building (figure 4) and the characteristic hallways that allowed surveillance of any attempted escape. One of the watchtowers (figure 5) resists the passing of time and abandon from a corner, but the majority of the iron of the passageways and doors has disappeared (figure 6).

The cell block where Vallejo stayed no longer exists, but the mute and dramatic solitary-confinement cells remain (figures 7, 8, and 9) in telling inscriptions that bear witness to long sentences with dates written on their inner walls. Sketches of Christ figures and saints, cutouts from magazines pinned to the walls, petitions and prayers eroding the plaster, the hammer crossed by a sickle: everything seems to be ready for the interpretation of the multiple motives and torments of the men who went through there. From inside one of the cells (figure 10), one can see a washbasin where the prisoners cleaned themselves and their clothes. It is in the courtyard that also lodges the only bathroom with its basic facility: a urinal at floor level and a toilet—also in the floor—that consisted of a hole with two footprints to stand on.

César Vallejo knew and suffered the harsh confinement of this Trujillo jail and his spirit would be forever marked: "The gravest moment of my life was my imprisonment in a jail of Peru."[2] Like *Trilce*, *Scales* reveals the scar of the poet after his imprisonment, rehashing some experiences explicitly and expressing his pain:

> Justice is not a human function. Nor can it be. Justice operates tacitly, deeper inside than all insides, in the courts and the prisoners. Justice—listen up, men of all latitudes!—is carried out in subterranean harmony, on the flipside of the senses and in the cerebral swings of street fairs. Hone down your hearts! Justice passes beneath every surface, behind everyone's backs. Lend subtler an ear to its fatal drumroll, and you will hear its only vigrant cymbal that, by the power of love, is smashed in two—its cymbal as vague and uncertain as the traces of the crime itself or of what is generally called crime.[3]

Just as in Trujillo his friends helped him to get out of prison, during his exile in Paris Vallejo received the support of fellow countrymen. Carlos

Godoy—the attorney we mentioned earlier—processed the pardon appearing after the numerous summonses sent by the Peruvian court, and from Spain, Pablo Abril de Vivero—diplomat and confidant—mediated in a grant so that he would receive a small economic sum with the objective of studying law in Madrid, which Vallejo did not do. The economic hardships suffered by César Vallejo in Paris were, at times, extreme and contributed to his unstable health. The dramatic and profound voice of the writer is in concordance with the personal vicissitudes and bellicose conflicts that emerged in Europe. Each year of exile brought a load of contrarieties to his indomitable character, as is reflected in a letter that he wrote to Pablo Abril on May 12, 1929: "As for me, I keep setting the pace perpetually standing still. My dilemma is the same every day: either I sell out or I go broke. And here I've held my ground because I'm already going broke."[4]

Beyond the contacts that he initiated with important intellectuals and the admiration that he stirred up among some writers—Gerardo Diego and José Bergamín handle the publication in Spain of the second edition of Trilce—he never found that longed-for ease, and the poverty was constant. Living with and then marrying Georgette Philippart did not change the course of that sometimes mendicant pilgrimage, and his support of communism added difficulties to his stay in France.

César Vallejo was immersed in the first half of the twentieth century, where the entire world was living through profound transformations. He lived the genesis of the South American political changes in direct contact with protagonists of his Peruvian homeland—Raúl Haya de la Torre and José Carlos Mariátegui, among others. He was an exile in an emblematic Paris that brought together the most important artists and writers of the time, and he participated enthusiastically in the defense of the Spanish Republic. Submerged in the landscapes that touched him, his poetic voice knew how to interpret these human fingerprints without giving up on an innovating and free spirit that produced some of the most brilliant poems in all of literature.

The ruins of the Trujillo jail, a mute and brutal testimony of pain, today are falling into rubble, while the Peruvian's writing, bringing together readers from different parts of the world, is proclaiming survival and transcendence:

Then all the humans on the earth
surrounded him; they looked at his sad corpse, moved;
he slowly got up,
hugged the first man; he went on his way....[5]

ANDRÉS ECHEVARRÍA
Montevideo

4. Prison corridor between cell blocks and perimeter wall. Photographer: Andrés Echevarría.

5. Remains of only watchtower still standing. Photographer: Andrés Echevarría.

6. Entrance to cell block and cell doorways.
Photographer: Andrés Echevarría.

7. Entrance to solitary-confinement cells and courtyard.
Photographer: Andrés Echevarría.

8. Solitary-confinement cell ruins and remains of courtyard.
Photographer: Andrés Echevarría.

9. Solitary-confinement cell doorways.
Photographer: Andrés Echevarría.

(*opposite*)
10. View from inside cell onto courtyard, with washbasin.
Photographer: Andrés Echevarría.

II

Time Time.
Noon clogged up nighttime fog.[6]
Boring pump of the cellblock backwashes
time time time time.

Was Was.

Roosters songsing[7] scratching in vain.
Clear day's mouth that conjugates
was was was was.

Tomorrow Tomorrow.

The warm repose of being though.
The present thinks hold on to me for
tomorrow tomorrow tomorrow tomorrow.

Name Name.

What calls all that puts on hedge us?[8]
It's called Thesame that suffers
name name name namE.[9]

XVIII

Oh the four walls of the cell.
Ah the four whitening walls
that irrefutably face the same number.

Breeding ground of nerves, evil breach,
through its four corners how it snaps
apart daily shackled extremities.

Loving keeper of innumerable keys,
if you were here, if you could see
unto what hour these walls are four.
Against them we'd be with you, just the two,
more two than ever. And you wouldn't even cry,
speak, liberator!

Ah the four walls of the cell.
Meanwhile as for those that hurt me, most
the two lengthy ones that tonight
have something of mothers who now
deceased each lead through bromined slides,[10]
a child by the hand.

And only will I keep my hold,
with my right hand, that makes do for both,
upraised, in search of a tertiary arm
that is to pupilate, between my where and when,
this stunted adulthood of man.[11]

XX

Flush with the beaten froth bulwarked
by ideal stone. Thus I barely
render 1 near 1 so as not to fall.

That mustachioed man. The sun,
his only wheel iron-rimmed, fifth and perfect,
and upwardly from it.
Clamor of crotch buttons
                free,
clamor that reprehends A vertical subordinate.
Juridical drainage. Pleasant prank.

But I suffer. Hereabouts I suffer. Thereabouts I suffer.

And here I am doting, I am
one beautiful person, when
williamthesecondary man
toils and sweats happiness
in gushes, putting a shine on the shoe
of his little three-year-old girl.

Shaggy cocks his head and rubs one side.
The girl meanwhile sticks her forefinger
on her tongue which starts spelling
the tangles of tangles of the tangles,
and she daubs the other shoe, secretly,
with an itty bit of silyba and dirt,[12]
            but only with,
             an itty bi-
              .t.

XLI

Death on its knees is spilling
white blood that isn't blood.
It smells of guarantee.
But already I want to laugh.

Something's murmured over there. They're quiet.
Someone whistles courage sideways,
and one might even count in pairs
twenty-three ribs that miss
each other, on both sides; one might count
in pairs as well, the whole line of trapezius guards.

Meanwhile, the policial drum-roller
(once again I want to laugh)
settles up and sticks it to us,
take that take that,
from membrane to membrane,
smack
after
smack.

L

  Cerberus four times
per day his padlock wields, opening
closing our sternums, with winks
we comprehend perfectly.

  With astounded melancholic breeches,
childish in transcendental disarray,
standing, the poor ole man is adorable.
He jokes with the prisoners, chockfull
the groins with jabs. And lunkhead even
gnaws on some crust for them; but always
just doing his job.

  In between the bars he sticks the fiscal
point, unseen, hoisting up the phalanx
of his pinky,
on the trail of what I say,
what I eat,
what I dream.
The raven wants there nevermore be insides,
and how we ache from this that Cerberus wants.

  In a clockwork system, the imminent,
pythagorean! ole man plays
breadthwise in the aortas. And only
from time to night, by night
he somewhat skirts his exception from metal.
But, naturally,
always just doing his job.

LVIII

In the cell, in the solid, the corners
as well huddle together.

I sort out the nudes that are wearing thin,
folding over, beraggled.[13]

I my panting horse dismount, fuming
lines with clouts and horizons;
a spumous foot against three hooves.
And I help him: Giddyup, animal!

Less might be taken, ever less, from what
I were obliged to apportion,
in the cell, in the liquid.

The prison mate was eating the wheat
from the knolls, with my own spoon,
when, at my parents' table, as a child,
I'd fallen asleep while chewing.

I whisper to him:
Come here, leave near the other corner:
beat it . . . beeline . . . bolt!

And inadvertently I adduce, plan,
nigh the worn-out devout bunk:
Don't believe it. That doctor was a healthy man.

I no longer will laugh when my mother prays
in childhood and on Sunday, at four
in the morning, for the wanderers,
prisoners,
sick,
and poor.

In the sheepfold of children, I no longer will aim
punches at anyone, who, afterward,
still bleeding, may cry: Next Saturday
I'll give you my cold cuts, just
don't hit me!
I won't say okay anymore.

In the cell, in the unlimited gas
until spinning in the condensation,
who's stumbling around outside?

LXI

Tonight I get down from my horse
at the door of the house, where
I bid farewell at the rooster's crow.
It's locked and no one responds.

The bench on which Mama had delivered
my older brother, so that he'd saddle
the backs I would ride bare,
through furrows and long hedges, country boy;
stone bench on which I've let my woebegone
infancy yellow in the sun ... And this woe
that frames the threshold?

God in foreign peace,
sneezes, as if also calling, the beast;
sniffs about, trotting on cobbles. Then doubt
whinnies,
wiggles a willing ear.

Must be Papa stayed up praying, and maybe
he thinks I'm running late.
My sisters, humming their fancies
bubbling homey,
preparing for the party that draws near
as now there's almost nothing missing.
I wait, I wait, my heart
an egg about to be laid, that gets stuck.

Numerous family that we left
not long ago, today no one waiting, nor even a taper
placed on the alter in light of our return.
Again I call, and nothing.
We fall silent and start to sob, and the animal
whinnies, still whinnies more.

Everyone's forever sleeping,
and their utmost doing, for at last
my horse wears out from nodding
in turn, half-asleep, to each assent, he says
that it's okay, that everything is A-okay.

LETTER TO *La Reforma*

Huamachuco, August 12, 1920

To the Editors of *La Reforma*, Trujillo
Dear Gentlemen,

Today I address the following words to *La Industria* of this city: Huamachuco, August 12, 1920. Dear gentlemen of *La Industria*, Trujillo. My dear gentlemen, in your prestigious newspaper's volume 7 of this month I have just read the charges being pressed and wired in by Carlos Santa María, of Santiago de Chuco, concerning the supposed fault of numerous gentlemen and my own fault for the fire and plundering that, according to the claimant, occurred in his commercial store in that city.

I am surprised by and amazed at slander as brutal as this, with which the aforesaid Santa María intends to bring me down. I energetically protest this and hereby invoke my rights in the face of such infamy before the justice system. I had no other choice. Let this Santa María beware of the legal repercussions for the despicable slander that today I denounce.

I respectfully request that you, gentlemen, publish the present letter.

Much obliged for your consideration, sincerely and without further requests at this time.

Yours truly,

César Vallejo

LETTER TO ÓSCAR IMAÑA

Trujillo, October 26, 1920

Dear Óscar,

I've read the last letter you wrote to Antenor. As I see from it, you're ruined by boredom and by Pacasmayo. It's the pits. Here you've got me as eaten away by monotony as you. What are we going to do, Óscar? Endure it, endure it.

I bet by now you've already received news that I'm being civilly prosecuted and criminally charged in Santiago de Chuco and also that I was sought after by the law at the doors of the Panopticon. There you have what I must endure to live. Now you see. So for two months now I've been in hiding, and for one month living in Mansiche with Antenor and Julio.

When are you coming by here, so we can laugh together until it hurts? God I wish you'd drop in for a bit. I think it's rather simple, just a matter of fifteen soles at most. Come on, get over here; don't be a lug.

Maybe in a few days the case will be solved, and will be solved in my favor. I find it hard to believe. But, maybe. I'll let you know what happens.

Probably within two months or so we'll set off on a trip outside of Peru with Antenor. Let's at least plan on it. As for me, I think it's a sure thing.

And you? When?

Before leaving, we'll plan to edit a book, a work by all of us in collaboration. It will be the crystallization of our fraternal life for so many years of our best childhood times. Send us your writings and let us know what suits you best, poems or prose. You'll choose. The book will be two hundred pages. It doesn't seem too bad now, does it?

I've just gone to sleep after lunch and have woken up with a bit of a cold.

Don't keep silent. Write to me always, by way of Antenor. I'm sorry that this isn't longer; I feel somewhat ill.

Highest regards.

César

POET VALLEJO JAILED IN TRUJILLO
REQUESTS SUPPORT OF LIMA'S INTELLECTUALS

From Trujillo Central Jail, the poet César Vallejo has addressed to us a moving letter, which our readers will find later.[14] They are bitter words through which we hear the screaming desperation of an artist who, with his freedom, reveals the frightful loss of his dignity and good name. Vallejo, whom many of us know, lived a long while in Lima, and his flawless conduct always earned him everyone's high regards. He worked in silence. He lived in silence. In silence he put on the page his wonderful poems: many of them rebellious, harsh, others arbitrary, but all of them the fruit of a robust mind and of the pure blood of a boy's beautiful heart.

How could such an upright and irreproachable man have suddenly ended up in a provincial jail?

The poets say that it's just a local feud. Mr. Haya de La Torre, ex-president of the Student Federation and Trujillo intellectual, confirms Vallejo's tortured protest. As we are cut off from Vallejo's current living situation, truly surprised by this painful news, we limit ourselves, with all sincerity, with all our love and faith, to demanding that all who can help shed light on this event, congressional representatives of Trujillo, students and writers of Lima, effectively step in, so that Vallejo—innocent, as we suppose—regains the freedom that he so passionately demands and that ignites such throbbing complaints.

Gastón Roger

[La Prensa (Lima), December 29, 1920]

LETTER TO GASTÓN ROGER

[Trujillo, December 1920][15]

My Dear Friend,

For the past month, I have been imprisoned in this city's jail, calamitously judged for a series of despicable crimes that I did not commit. It is this provincial environment. The misguided distrust of local slander: I am from the heartland. I am now a victim of one out of so many gratuitous or brutally cajoled infamies that abound, reeking of bats, in every heap of district affairs. For I am from the same land as those who accuse me, and I passed through Santiago de Chuco, months ago, when there were killings and fires in that province. It is this provincial environment. That is all.

And what is more, I have been prosecuted with utter impunity and utter impudence. And, as now I am in grave danger of being found guilty by the criminal court, one of these days, I hope that you, who valued something in my artistic work, may want to show, along with the rest of our friends in Lima, some gesture of sympathy and of interest in my favor, on the occasion of this outrage and this mortal wound, by which they want to victimize me, indifferent to my innocence and the law. I would imagine that this thoughtfulness, on your part, would lead to the acquittal to which I have a right in the case at hand.

The days are numbered until the hearing, and I am almost sure of the compassion with which this fraternal petition will be received by the resilient intelligentsia of Lima.

Affectionately yours,

César Vallejo

A few lines to demand that intellectuals and newspapers of Lima give the generous warmth of their support to the poet César Vallejo, locked up today in a cell of Trujillo Central Jail by order of the provincial court of a remote Andean town in the north.

After long years of absence, Vallejo journeyed to his homeland, along with his omens and success, an offering of grief at the grave of his deceased mother. That's where he was met by the endless, traditional, and slithering local feud that culminates in a sordid ambush, a large-scale attack and swift shyster lawyering, the sealed envelope, the penal code, and the slammer. Now, accused of a thousand crimes, the poet, rebel in art and rhythm, already a master of his own new luminous way, has been handcuffed, defeated, and transferred to the Trujillo penitentiary.

Confused with criminals and degenerates, with bandits and crooks, César A. Vallejo, one of the few souls I can honestly say is good and one of the few talents worth admiring without reservation, waits in his cell for a mistaken and perhaps unacceptable ruling, "in view" of a sinister investigation file in which he's accused of homicide, arson, sedition, and robbery.

The singer of *The Black Heralds* is screaming from his prison: "They're trying to kill my youth, which is the only thing I hold present and cherish." His bitterly sincere voice reminds us that Vallejo is poor and modest. Isn't his pain a call to collective action in his favor for all of us who know him?

Let us remember his youth, the high value of his vigorous mind, the pain of his life as a restless, humble dreamer and let us direct our encouraging voice to the shackled poet. As for the judges, we need not call for their clemency, since this is unnecessary when one is innocent; suffice an appeal to their spiritual superiority and sense of humanity, regulator of all justice.

Chorrillos, 1920

Víctor Raúl Haya de La Torre

[*La Prensa* (Lima), December 20, 1920]

PETITION OF
UNIVERSIDAD DE TRUJILLO STUDENTS

Hon. President of the Supreme Court of Justice:

A nondeferrable duty to humanity, a pressing obligation of comradery
and spiritual solidarity among students, a high moral imperative, and
an even higher imperative of Justice forces us to sign this petition that
we bring before you today through your esteemed authority, before the
respectable and most honorable body over which you preside and guarantee the codes of Justice and human rights, to plead, in the name of
the university students of Trujillo, for the acquittal of the distinguished
poet and our schoolmate, Mr. César A. Vallejo, who has been vulgarly en-
tangled in the events of Santiago de Chuco from last August. With complete certainty of the defendant's high moral stature, with a comprehensive understanding of his personal background unblemished to date, we
appeal to Your Honor's higher conscience, developed to an eminent degree, and that of the distinguished magistrates that constitute this court;
we appeal to the free, incorruptible conscience, inaccessible to any solici-
tation beyond the jurisdiction of law and justice; we appeal to the higher
conscience capable of liberating itself from the dead word, from the petrified skeleton of a code, which, like all entities that perform a function of
vital importance, flows over the limited and exiguous shores of an official
record, all fabrication, always insufficient, a written process that cannot
at all translate the complex substantiality of the facts, which is powerless
when it comes to translating lived fluid reality with absolute integrity. It
is in the familiar fraternity of the classroom, in the daily contact, and in
cordial proximity of our studies that a stronger sense of one's compo-
sition and worth can be attained, along with one's ethical compass, respect for the law, honor, and purity of a youthful life. On this occasion,
no other source seems more efficient or of more informatively loyal value.
César A. Vallejo always was, as his professors and classmates will attest,
an example of responsibility, progress, and morality—singular conditions that have allowed him to achieve the most exceptional distinctions
during the course of his university studies. Therefore, when applied to
uninhibited logic, the decision of serene and higher reasoning, it is im-

plausible that an entire life of persistent and thorough effort would suddenly decide to commit a despicable crime, would add to that a degrading stigma, the ignominious and shameful stain of a prison sentence.

In making this petition, the youth of the university do nothing more than gather a general desire, a decision of public conscience that has erupted with resounding spontaneity, with regard to the person of CÉSAR VALLEJO, which, as in all countries of advanced juridical culture, constitutes a symptomatic fact to determine the groundlessness of an accusation and the stay or acquittal of the charged person.

In view of the foregoing reasons of high spiritual order, the undersigned entrust the higher juridical sense of the respectable magistrates who constitute the court and, on this occasion, have the singular honor of paying their respects and homage to the illustrious and sacred practice that they perform at the core of our society.

Trujillo, December 3, 1920
Signed by:
Álvaro Pinillos Goicochea, Leoncio Muñoz Rázuri, Juan de Dios Ganoza, Carlos Manuel Cox, Arcesio Condemarín, Alberto Larco, Carlos Espejo Asturrizaga, Leopoldo H. Ortiz, Juan Manuel Sotero, Víctor Manuel Zavaleta, C. Gerardo Vásquez Batistini, Víctor Cárcamo, José Gálvez Cárdenas, Manuel J. Acevedo, Carlos E. Colcochea, Antenor Guerra García, Manuel A. Villacorta Corcuera, Alberto Mannucci, Enrique Benites Loayza, Nicanor León Díaz, A. Alvarez León, Luis A. Arbulú, Enrique Aruajo C., José M. Godoy, José María Peña Aranda, G. Torres Rivas, Agustín Orrego H., Emiliano Castañeda Albites, Manuel Mondoñedo B., Mario N. Saldaña A., César A. Alfaro, F. A. Galarreta, Manuel Vásquez Díaz, José Gabriel Del Castillo, Leonidas Gayoso, A. Linch Urteaga, Diógenes M. Vásquez, Ricardo R. Cabrera, Luciano M. Castillo C., José Salomé Díaz, M. Rodríguez, J. C. La Cunza, Alfredo Rebaza Acosta, D. Cedrón C., Augustín P. Masías, Leonidas J. Risco, Francisco Carranza, F. Moreno M., Jorge Guimaraes B., M. J. Revilla, Max Benites Loayza, Humberto S. Vásquez, Sergio Cuba Torres, Carlos F. Mendoza, Alfredo Otoya Porturas, Carlos J. Calderón, and F. Esquerre Cedrón.

PETITION OF
TRUJILLO JOURNALISTS

Hon. President of the Criminal Court:

The journalists of Trujillo shall not remain silent at a time when the presence of a spiritual duty demands their collective voice, to make a plea in solidarity and cooperation to the high court over which you preside with such dignity. Few and far between are the events that merit a call to joint action, with full justification, of the journalists who, as an organ of public sentiment, are obligated to register that sentiment with integrity and fidelity. The undersigned persons of this petition believe that the occasion has arisen to exercise this function of solidarity and to demand, to you and before the criminal court, the absolution in favor of writer and poet César A. Vallejo, who has been embroiled in the criminal activities that occurred last August in Santiago de Chuco. Aware of the instruction that we exercise on the spiritual life of the country, aware of the human role that we assume with regard to our social organization, we shall not avoid the fulfillment of a duty and the exercise of a right, whose verification gives the measure of our public conscience and our collective responsibility. In the press, as in no other organization, the degree of ethical responsibility is made manifest and evident, more for what it silences and deprives than for what it makes explicit. Its greatest sin is omission, that is, to refrain from expressing what must be expressed in due time, to refrain from registering what at each hour of each day is demanding justice. The trial and imprisonment of CÉSAR VALLEJO has generated a vibrant sentiment that has already begun to transform, and we think that it is incompatible with our dignity as humans and journalists to mute our voice of solidarity, taking responsibility for a cowardly moral senselessness, in the face of our own conscience and the conscience of the collective. The undersigned of this petition, as mindful beings making use of the most unobjectionable and pure manifestation of inner freedom, often differ in political opinions or in the evaluation of daily events in our national or local life, but there is a higher plane of agreement, an ethical nexus of common accord that imposes on us a sort of emotional unity, which gives us a determined collective personality, beneath whose orientation a unanimity and concordance of thought and action is possible. A longing for pure justice, exempt from all the usual interests that distort and stray human opinion, has given rise to that elevated plane of concordance and has made it possible for our voice to obtain solidarity in a public act, which we judge to be of high professional and collective morality. It is, in view of this higher reality, which, as we said, constitutes the purest and freest aspect of our ethical personality and in which deliberations of the most powerful vitality of social sentiment get registered, that the undersigned journalists are incapable of remaining indifferent with regard to an individual case of justice that must, by force, and in fact does, directly, entail the justice of the collective.

Trujillo, December 15, 1920

Signed by:

Antenor Orrego, director of *La Reforma*, Carlos Manuel Cox, editor of *La Reforma*, G. Torres Rivas, editor of *La Reforma*, J. N. Vallejo, director of *La Libertad*, Luis Armas, editor of *La Libertad*, R. Haya, director of *La Industria*, José Eulogio Garrido, editor of *La Industria*, and Francisco Sandoval, editor of *La Reforma*.

LETTER TO ÓSCAR IMAÑA

Trujillo, February 12, 1921

Óscar,

Today I put down these lines for you from prison still. How about that? Oh, how I would've liked to write you with news of my release, but these attorneys!

I know that by now you're in Pacasmayo. And yet I know that you've got to let yourself out of the moment-to-moment to come by here. I hope that you do, and they let me go to Salaverry to wrap my arms around you.

Two public prosecutors have argued for my release, and the court even today has yet to hand down a ruling on my case. Not even because Morales sits on the bench. Clericalism is more than wretched.

You can imagine how I'm faring. At times I lose my patience and everything grows dark; very rarely am I well. I've got four months in prison under my belt, and now they must weaken my hardest fortresses.

We received the memorial from the ladies of Chiclayo. Today I'm writing a telegram to Cornejo's wife, expressing my thanks for such a considerate gesture.

In my cell I read every once in a while, and, in brief, I brood and gnaw my elbows out of rage, not exactly because of that honor thing but because of the material privation, completely material and my animal freedom. Óscar, this is awful.

I also write from time to time, and if any sweet breath fills my soul, it's the light of memory. . . . Oh the memory in prison! How it gets here and falls upon the heart, which it oils with melancholy already so decomposed. . . .

In short, I don't know what these people will do. We soon shall see.

Your brother,

César

IMPRISONMENT OF CÉSAR VALLEJO
IN TRUJILLO JAIL
EXPLAINS THE CAUSES OF HIS IMPRISONMENT

The public is aware of the imprisonment suffered by the well-known Trujillo poet, César A. Vallejo, whose absence has been felt in this capital since he produced outstanding literary work with the publication of his book *The Black Heralds*. One will also recall the movement of sympathy to which the occasion of his unjustified detention gave rise.

A few days ago, Vallejo arrived at the capital, now free of the trumped charges that were sullying his good name; and, as we were interested in finding out the truth about his imprisonment and the causes behind it, yesterday we obtained the following information from him, which we now share with our readers:

"I was released from prison on the twenty-sixth of last February. The criminal court ruled that there was no case against me for the crime of arson, but that there was for the other less serious crimes, whose maximum punishment of detention I had served at the time this ruling was handed down.

"I am utterly shocked by the savage events that occurred in Santiago de Chuco in August; my conscience and the public outcry attest. I was accused with utter certainty and despicable slander, for no other reason than resentment and revenge proper to provincial politics, to which some of my brothers who reside in the north are now falling victim. For the respective summary trial, the Trujillo Court commissioned a judge ad hoc, Elías Iturri, who scandalously and fraudulently bilked the preliminary investigation, committing every sort of legicide[16] to fulfill a previously established corrupt agreement to implicate the most notable residents of the area and, especially, to implicate me.

"Iturri has had and still has a good backer in the heart of the criminal court to hear his proceedings, and this explains how that preliminary investigation has been approved in plain discord with all law and conscience. I hereby affirm and sustain this. Not even Francis of Assisi would receive a fair ruling from a judicial system in the provinces! There, justifications — perhaps all of them — are immoral and perverted, while pettifogging shysters stuff their guts and frocks, aided by impunity.

"My case has gone to the Supreme Court of Appeals. I hope that this high judicial body will clarify all that preliminary legal investigation, finding me far removed from those savage crimes in Santiago de Chuco, serious or minor as they may be. By supposing that I took part in them, the Trujillo Court intends to justify to the public its decision to keep me imprisoned arbitrarily for so long and at the same time to corroborate its act by a judge, a very juridical and rather creole shuffle.

"In closing, I would like to take this opportunity to publicly recognize the intellectuals of Peru for the words of respect that they have offered on the occasion of my imprisonment and, in particular, the journalists who have treated me so nobly."

With these words from the author of *The Black Heralds*, we say good-bye, outstretching our hands to him.

[*La Crónica* (Lima), May 8, 1921]

NOTES

INTRODUCTION

1. For more on this antinomy, see my paper, "El arte de ir en contra: La vanguardia histórica y el programa emulador de César Vallejo" (Flores Heredia and Echevarría 2016, 304–15).

2. See González Vigil 2013a, 12.

3. For an in-depth analysis of the early critical reception of *Scales*, see González Montes 2002, 61–80.

4. Tárvara Córdova 2014. El Congreso Internacional Vallejo Siempre revealed unmistakable interest in Vallejo's prose narrative, as demonstrated by the lectures "Creciente interés de la crítica por la narrativa de Vallejo (1992–2014)," by Antonio González Montes; "Diversidad sociocultural y racionalidades en El *tungesteno*," by Edith Pérez Orozco; "El primer cuento marxista para niños en el Perú: El caso de 'Paco Yunque,' de César Vallejo," by Jorge Valenzuela Garcés; "César Vallejo: *Sabiduría*, una novela trunca e inconclusa," by José Luis Ayala; "*Fabla salvaje*, de César Vallejo: Más acá del complejo edípico," by Macedonio Villafán Broncano; "Violencia y marginalidad en la narrativa de César Vallejo para niños y jóvenes," by Sanie E. Lozano Alvarado; and "Dialogismo y literatura: Una relectura de la narrativa de Vallejo," by Miguel Ángel Huamán.

5. To commemorate the passing, Vallejo wrote the elegy "To My Dead Brother," which he first published in the magazine *Cultura Infantil* in August 1917, only to then rework it as "To My Brother Miguel" and place it in the section "Songs of Home" of the book *The Black Heralds*.

6. Hart 2013, 43.

7. See XVIII, XXIII, XXVIII, LII, LVIII, and LXV, *Trilce*, in González Vigil 2013b; "Más allá de la vida y la muerte," *Escalas*, in González Vigil 2013a; and "Lánguidamente su licor," *Contra el secreto profesional* in De Priego, 508.

8. See "César Vallejo, del laberinto vital a la obra" (Flores Heredia 2014, 264).

9. See Puccinelli, 49–53.

10. See César Vallejo, "Against Professional Secrets" (Puccinelli, 421–25; Mulligan, 164–67); "Defense of Life" (Puccinelli, 336–37; Mulligan, 154–55); "Artists Facing Politics" (Puccinelli 517–19; Mulligan 172–73); and "Literature behind Closed Doors" (Puccinelli, 599–601; Mulligan, 186–88).

11. See Hart 2007, 691, 700.

12. Patrón Candela, 334–36.

13. Ibid., 350, 352.

14. González Montes 2014b, 18.

15. See Antenor Orrego, "Palabras prologales a *Trilce*" (Silva-Santisteban and Moreano 1997), 169–78.

16. See Vallejo's letter to Pablo Abril de Vivero, July 24, 1927 (Cabel 2002, 239–40; Mulligan 303–4).

17. See González Montes 2014b, 17.

18. Silva-Santisteban and Moreano 1997, xvi.

19. See César Vallejo, "Anniversary of Baudelaire" (Puccinelli, 611–12; Mulligan 190–91).

20. González Vigil 2013a, 11.

21. Ibid., 9–10.

22. Oviedo y Pérez de Tudela, 369.

23. Higgins, 230. See also "Languidly His Liqueur" (De Priego, 508–9; Mulligan, 225–26).

24. See Gutiérrez Girardot, 714–15.

25. Ibid., 715.

26. Vallejo's trajectory through the gothic strain of the romantic tradition can also be appreciated in his adoption of the theme of double identity in "Mirtho." For more on this, see González Montes 2014b, 23.

27. Gutiérrez Girardot, 717.

28. See César Vallejo "Serie y contrapunto" (Silva-Santisteban and Moreano 1999, 465–71).

29. See González Vigil 2013a, 12–14, for a strong synthesis of Neale-Silva's main lines of investigation. For the impact of Neale-Silva's research on literary criticism of Vallejo's prose fiction, see González Montes 2014a, 294–96.

30. Neale-Silva, 37–38.

31. The break from analogy stands as a trademark of avant-gardism and opens the possibility of experimental modalities, such as collage and the focus on the image, and preference for the oxymoron or the hypallage, that is, the extrapolation of paradox. For more, see Oviedo y Pérez de Tudela, 369.

32. González Vigil 2013a, 13.

33. Neale-Silva, 38.

34. Coyné, 48.

35. See Neale-Silva, 38.

36. See González Vigil 2013a, 14. Vallejo makes reference to Dostoevsky's writings in "Defense of Life" (Puccinelli, 336–37; Mulligan, 154–55); "Artists Facing Politics" (Puccinelli 517–19; Mulligan 172–73); and "Negations of Negations" (De Priego, 496; Mulligan, 202), inter alia.

37. Neale-Silva, 38–39.

38. González Vigil 2013a, 14.

39. See González Montes 2014b, 20. See also Augusto Monterroso, "The Dinosaur," in *Complete Works and Other Stories*, trans. Edith Grossman (Austin: University of Texas Press, 1995, 42). "The Dinosaur" in its entirety reads, "When he awoke, the dinosaur was still there."

THIS EDITION

1. See Couffon 1988.

2. Cf. Rolland et al. Also included in this edition of *Commune* are texts by Luis Aragon, Martin Andersen-Nexö, Paul Nizan, Claude Morgan, Jaime Cortesão, Langston Hughes, Pyotr Pavlenko, and Joseph Billiet, among others.

3. The Couffon manuscript is available in González Vigil 2013a and Silva-Santisteban and Moreano 1999.

4. The first attempt at a comprehensive biography in English has recently been made by Stephan Hart 2013.

SCALES

1. **vigrant** Meo Zilio suggests that *vagoroso* (*vago* + -*roso*) is based on an analogical pattern with *vaporoso* (vaporous) and a psychological impulse of *vagaroso* (vagrant) + *vigoroso* (vigorous) (276). Neale-Silva interprets the neologism based on *vagaroso* (vagrant) and *vigoroso* (vigorous) (1975, 153). We prefer "vigrant" as a way to extend the neologistic use by applying Neale-Silva's insight into the sense of "vigor."

2. **alvine** In anatomy, *alvino* (alvine) refers to that which is of or related to the lower intestine. However, Vallejo is taking advantage of the homophony between *alvino* and *albino* (albino). This word also appears in poem XXVI of *Trilce*. See González Vigil 2013b, 265.

3. **insaharates** Forcing the noun *Sahara* into a verb (*ensahara*), Vallejo describes thirst as a desert that spreads through the mouth.

4. **thricey** In the expression *esos sonidos trágicos y treses*, Vallejo pluralizes the noun *tres* (three) and assigns it an adjectival value. Besides "thricey," another possible translation could be "threely."

5. **ovoe** In the phrase *una suave cadera de óvoe*, Vallejo appears to have replaced the "b" of *éboe* (oboe) with a "v," a play that is not uncommon to his writing from this period. For example, see poem IX in *Trilce* (González Vigil 2013b, 233–34; Mulligan, 49).

6. **loudspoken . . . chatty glassware** The Castilian phrase, *altopado al remate de todos los vasos comunicantes*, poses several challenges to translation. First, the coined word *altopado* modifies the third sound that Vallejo is describing. We interpret *altopado* to derive from *altoparlante* (loudspeaker,) at the risk of overclarifying what is quite opaque in the source. Additionally, while *vasos comunicantes* are "communicating vessels" in the technical sense, we agree with Neale-Silva that "technical and scientific terms have no taxonomical or clarifying function in Vallejo's poetry. Incorporated into the reign of poetry, they transform into tropes" (1971, 545). In light of this, we have preferred to expose the metaphorical quality of *vasos comunicantes* with "chatty glassware" rather than employing the more obvious "communicating vessels."

7. **yaraví** This refers to a sweet and melancholic song of Incan origin that is played with the *quena*, or Andean fife.

8. **angular brass of my shaved face** When Vallejo refers to *los angulosos cobres de mi rostro rasurado*, he is evoking the mineral copper and, by pluralizing the noun, the brass section of an orchestra. This is similar to what he has done with *coro de vientos*. For more on this, see the introduction to this volume.

9. **antara** An *antara* is a type of Andean flute, a pan flute.

10. **for ever and never** In Castilian *por siempre jamás* contains a similar inherent contradiction.

11. **scope out** It is not clear what Vallejo means by *arcenan*. Given the context, it appears to express the act of "looking," perhaps with hints of "scoping," given the phonetic proximity of *arcenar* to "arsenal."

12. **carabids** While the Castilian word *cárabos* might also be translated as some sort of an owl, which would seem appropriate given the context of being watched over, the ground beetle "carabid" seems like a better fit, since these are insectivorous, which seems to rhyme thematically with the psychological cannibalism that goes on between Palomino and the other inmates.

13. **greatocean** Vallejo coins the adjective *grandeocéano*, fusing *grande* (big, grand) and *océano* (ocean).

14. **echoed** In Castilian Vallejo forces the noun *eco* (echo) into the past participle *ecado* and assigned it an adjectival function, rather than using *resonado*, which would more or less cover the same semantic ground.

15. **what frozen shoulders** In Castilian Vallejo writes, *"qué amargos calabazas le florecían"* (literally, what bitter pumpkins were flourishing from him), where the image of the *calabaza* evokes the phrase *dar calabazas* (to brush off). We've modified the idiomatic phrase "cold shoulder" to operate metaphorically in way parallel to what we see in the source.

16. **subjunct her golden aqueous name** Vallejo seems to be playing off the tradition in many Hispanic countries, in which a married woman's last name would be followed by *de* (of) and then the last name of her husband. Thus, if Nérida marries Walter Wolcot, her last name becomes "del Mar de Wolcot." Vallejo puns on her *aqueous* name (*mar* also means "sea") and also on the dependency of one name on the other. With the neologism *subjuntivar*, Vallejo seems to be fusing *sujetar* (subdue) and *subjuntivo* (subjunctive) to arrive at a meaning of "to subordinate."

17. **now at his wounded soul . . . moons of absence** There is highly poetic manipulation of language in these lines. First, Vallejo intimates the parallelism with a prepositional phrase (*now at his soul, now*) but then disrupts it by subordinating the main clause ("now that"). Second, he employs the phrase *ocasos moscardados de recuerdos*, where *moscardado* is a neologism that appears to be based on *moscarda*, which, according to the *Diccionario de la lengua española*, refers to the bluebottle fly (genus *Calliphora*), as well as *cresa*, that is, "larva" or "the eggs of the queen bee." Vallejo has forced the noun into a past participle and assigned it an adjectival function. Finally,

he prefers the Portuguese/Galician term *saudad* rather than its Spanish derivation (*soledad*) so as to capture the rich meaning of the "presence of absence."

18. **only from time to late . . . inwindow** Vallejo writes *sólo de vez en tarde*, literally, "only from time to late" (rather than *solo de vez en cuando* or "only from time to time"). Additionally, he coins the verb *enventenar*, apparently following the morphological pattern of *inventar* (to invent) with a semantic influence of *ventana* (window).

19. The shifts in tense follow Vallejo's.

20. **towerful** Vallejo's use of the adjective *torreada*, which describes an area filled with towers, is irregular and appears to qualify music with the height of a building. This play is so evident in the Castilian that we believe the neologism "towerful" is justified.

21. **greenbottle** Vallejo qualifies Wolcot's eyes as *verdebotella*, playing off the *mosca verde botella* (greenbottle fly).

22. The shift in tense follows Vallejo's. For more on this narrative strategy, see González Montes 2002, 206–8.

23. **whitecapped** Vallejo forces *cabrillear* (to form white caps in the sea) into the adjective *cabrilleantes* to describe the madwoman's eyes.

24. **spiderwebbed** Vallejo additionally qualifies the woman's eyes as *entelarañados*, an adjective based on *telaraña* (spider web), perhaps with a psychological impulse from *enmarañar* (to tangle).

25. **cleversed** Vallejo coins the adjective *artimañoso* in the phrase "*con artimañoso desvío del gusto.*" The neologism appear to have been derived from *artimaña* (skill) and *mañoso* (cunning).

26. **carnature** Vallejo writes *carnatura*, which appears to be a neologism based on *carne* (flesh, meat) and *natura* (nature), but clearly with an impulse to rhyme with *nervadura* a couple of lines later.

27. **tubulated** Vallejo writes *tubulado*, which appears to fuse *tubular* (tubular) with *tabulado* (tabulated).

28. **calembour** It's interesting to note that Vallejo preferred the French *calembour* over the Spanish *calembur* the year before he moved to Paris.

29. **porcelained** Vallejo coins the adjective *aporcelanadas*, which appears to derive from *porcelana* (porcelain). The word here seems to give the "soul" and "pituitaries" of the narrator's friend a sense of fragility.

30. **bronzemongery** The Castilian word *broncería* refers to a collection of bronze pieces. A close rendering in English is "ironmongery," though, for our translation, we have preferred to incorporate "bronze," since this substance contains strong cultural connotations (i.e., *la raza de bronce*) and because we know that the provisional title of *Trilce*—written during the same period as *Scales*—was *Cráneos de bronce*.

31. **edgility** Vallejo uses the neologism *aristaje*, forming an abstract noun by applying the ending -*aje* to the noun *arista* (edge). While this word formation is per-

fectly in agreement with Castilian morphology, it is not recognized by the Real Academia Española.

32. **hexagonned** Vallejo coins the word *exagonados*. Instead of using the adjectival form (either *hexagonal* or *exagonal*) he imparts a new verbal emphasis on the word by adding the ending *-ado*, giving the function of a passive participle employed as an adjective.

33. **personage whose goatee seemed to be dripping** Vallejo characterizes the man as a *personaje de biscotelas chorreantes*. *Biscotela* is very light semisweet bread, often served to accompany coffee or tea. The poet appears to be making a homophonic play by replacing *bigotes* with *bizcotelas*. We have veered away from the text to conserve the clarity of the image.

APPENDIX

1. Cabel 2011, 239.
2. *Poemas humanos* 1961, 91.
3. González Vigil 2013b, 74.
4. Ibid. 2013a, 92.
5. *Poemas humanos* 1961, 131.
6. **nighttime fog** The Castilian word *relente* refers to dew or fog that appears in the night or to the bright glare of the sun, reflected or not, that forces onlookers to advert their gaze. The sense of repulsion is strong here, but the notion that "noon" contains the fog from the night before seems coherent with the pump that "backwashes" time.

7. **songsing** Vallejo verbalizes the noun *canción*, probably following the morphology of *cantar* (to sing).

8. **What calls all that puts on hedge us** This very idiosyncratic line reads thusly in the Castilian: *¿Qué se llama cuanto heriza nos?* In the beginning of the expression we find the odd phrase *qué se llama* instead of the expected *cómo se llama* (what does one call). Moreover, according to Meo Zilio, *heriza nos* shows a psychological impulse of *herir* (to wound) and thus grafts the image of the *herida* (wound) onto the word; the syntactic inversion of the position of *nos* is added to the viewable effect of prosthesis, aimed at concentrating the shuddering action of *erizar* (to bristle) upon the passive subject of *nos* (253–54). Larrea suggests that the attachment of the h to *erizar* "evokes the presence of various expressions of bristling [raising hairs on end]: horrendous, horrible, horrify and horripilate" (in González Vigil 1991, 231). To account for the neologism, the phrase "to put on edge" has been modified with "hedge" to evoke the spiny hedgehog (i.e., the bristling), and the syntactical inversion has likewise been recreated.

9. **Thesame . . . namE** The word *Lomismo* is a contraction of *lo mismo* (the same). The capitalization of the final *e* in "namE" imitates Vallejo's *nombrE*.

10. **bromined slides** In the phrase *bromurados declives* we find the neologism

bromurados, where Vallejo seems to have fused *bromuro* (bromide) with *amurallado* (walled, fortified). It is our sense that the neologism results in a meaning of "vein" or "streak," running through the "slides" that the mother and child cross.

11. **stunted adulthood of man** The line *mayoría inválida de hombre* encapsulates a major idea to which Vallejo returns time and again through *Trilce* and other works as well: the idea of reaching one's potential. As Martos and Villanueva point out, by the end of the poem the narrator "is not even left with the image of his mother; he is in search of a 'terciario brazo': be it the Beloved or any other human being who may symbolize protection, tutelage, help. He is an adult, but is also disabled [*inválido*]. He is an imploring man-child" (125). Ferrari perceives an "obsession with the mother and with the feeling of mutilation that awakens the consciousness of adulthood in the poet. . . . The final line, which is an extension of 'Dios' and 'Desnudo en barro' in *Los heraldos negros*, clarifies the sense of the whole poem. It is the outcry of the orphan, the mutilated, one-armed heart, which looks for the third protective presence, the mother perhaps, the new mother" (122, 124). For Escobar, at the end of the poem, "this action of affective interest is projected upon the 'donde' and 'cuando' (i.e., space and time) of the man who is suffering a *mayoría inválida de hombre*, whose full human condition, despite being an adult, is cut off and damaged" (105–6). Most English translations render this line as "invalid majority of man"; however, *mayoría* is not only "majority" but the state of being a *mayor* (adult), that is, adulthood. The sense of coming up short, of not reaching completion, the repeating odd number throughout *Trilce* here takes the form of an adulthood that exists only as a horizon.

12. **with an itty bit of silyba and dirt** Vallejo prefers *saliba* over *saliva*, as a way to evoke the language of the little girl shining the shoes of her convicted father. A similar gesture is made at the end of the poem, where the sound of spitting is evoked graphically.

13. **beraggled** According to Meo Zilio, the verbal neologism *se harapan* is based on *harapo* (rag, tatter), following an analogical pattern and psycholinguistic impulse from the word *arroparse* (wrap up, tuck in) (280–81). We have played on "bedraggled" to evoke the rags seen in the source.

14. Gastón Roger (pseudonym of Ezequiel Balarezo Pinillos and chronicler of *La Prensa* in Lima) published this letter in the evening edition of that newspaper on December 29, 1920.

15. This letter was published on December 29, 1920, in *La Prensa*, but it is unclear on which day of his incarceration Vallejo actually wrote it.

16. In Spanish Vallejo writes *todo género de legicidios*, coining the word *legicidio*, following the morphological pattern of *homocidio*, with the meaning of "murder of the law."

SELECTED BIBLIOGRAPHY

WORKS BY CÉSAR VALLEJO

Artículos y crónicas completos. Vols. 1–2. Edited by Jorge Puccinelli. Lima: Pontificia Universidad Católica del Perú, 2002.

Cartas de César Vallejo a Pablo Abril de Vivero. Edición facsimilar. Prologue by Andrés Echevarría. Montevideo: Biblioteca Nacional de Uruguay, 2013.

The Complete Poetry: A Bilingual Edition; César Vallejo. Edited and translated by Clayton Eshleman. Berkeley: University of California Press, 2007.

Correspondencia completa. Edited by Jesús Cabel. Lima: Pontificia Universidad Católica del Perú, 2002.

Correspondencia completa. Edited by Jesús Cabel. Valencia: Pre-Textos, 2011.

Ensayos y reportajes completos. Edited by Manuel Miguel de Priego. Lima: Pontificia Universidad Católica del Perú, 2002.

Escalas. Lima: Talleres Tipográficos de la Penitenciaría, 1923.

Escalas melografiadas. Edited by Claude Couffon. Arequipa: Universidad Nacional de San Agustin, 1994.

Narrativa completa. Edited by Antonio Merino. Madrid: Akal, 1996.

Narrativa completa. Edited by Ricardo González Vigil. Lima: Copé, 2013a.

Narrativa completa. Edited by Ricardo Silva-Santisteban and Cecilia Moreano. Lima: Pontificia Universidad Católica del Perú, 1999.

Novelas: Tungsteno, Fabla salvaje, Escalas melografías. Edited by Jorge Falcón. Lima: Hora del Hombre, 1948.

Novelas y cuentos completos. Edited by Georgette de Vallejo. Lima: Moncloa, 1967.

Obras completas. Vol. 1, *Obra poética.* Edited by Ricardo González Vigil. Lima: Centenario, 1991.

Poemas humanos: España, aparta de mí este cáliz. Buenos Aires: Losada, 1961.

Poesía completa. Edited by Ricardo González Vigil. Lima: Copé, 2013b.

Poesía completa. Vol. 2. Edited by Ricardo Silva-Santisteban and Cecilia Moreano. Lima: Pontificia Universidad Católica del Perú, 1997.

Selected Writings of César Vallejo. Edited by Joseph Mulligan. Middlebury: Wesleyan University Press, 2015.

Teatro Completo. Vol. 1. Edited by Ricardo Silva-Santisteban and Cecilia Moreano. Lima: Pontificia Universidad Católica del Perú, 1999.

WORKS ON CÉSAR VALLEJO

Barrera, Trinidad. "Escalas melografiadas o la lucidez vallejiana." *Cuadernos Hispanoamericanos. Homenaje a César Vallejo* 1, no. 454–55 (1988): 317–28.

Chirinos, Jorge Prado. "Una carta desconocida de César Vallejo." *Lexis* 16, no. 2 (1992): 259–66.

Clayton, Michelle. *Poetry in Pieces: César Vallejo and Lyric Modernity.* Berkeley: University of California Press, 2011.

Couffon, Claude. "Escalas melografiadas, un cuerpo vivo." In Couffon 1994, 11–18.

———. "Una versión inédita de *Escalas.*" In *La escritura de lo real: Cincuentenario de Vallejo,* edited by Nadine Ly, 39–44. Madrid: Ediciones de la Torre, 1988.

Coyné, André. "César Vallejo: Vida y obra." *Visión del Perú,* no. 4 (1969): 44–56.

Eschevarría, Andrés. "César Vallejo, del laberinto vital a la obra." In *Vallejo siempre,* edited by Gladys Flores Heredia, 2:261–69. Lima: Cátedra Vallejo, 2014.

Escobar, Alberto. *Cómo leer a Vallejo.* Lima: Villanueva, 1973.

Ferrari, Américo. *El universo poético de César Vallejo.* Lima: Heraldo, 1997.

Flores Heredia, Gladys, ed. *Vallejo 2014: Actas del Congreso Internacional Vallejo Siempre.* Lima: Cátedra Vallejo, 2014.

Flores Heredia, Gladys, and Andrés Echevarría, eds. *Vallejo 2016: Actas del Congreso Internacional Vallejo Siempre.* Lima: Cátedra Vallejo, 2016.

González Montes, Antonio. "Creciente interés de la crítica literaria por la narrativa de Vallejo (1992–2014)." In Flores Heredia 2014a, 291–309.

———. *Escalas hacia la modernización narrativa.* Lima: Fondo Editorial Universidad Nacional Mayor de San Marcos, 2002.

———. *Introducción a la narrativa de Vallejo.* Lima: Cátedra Vallejo, 2014b.

———. "La narrativa de César Vallejo." In *Intensidad y altura,* edited by Ricardo González Vigil, 221–264. Lima: Pontificia Universidad Católica del Perú, 1993.

Gutiérrez Girardot, Rafael. "La obra narrativa de César Vallejo." *Anales de Literatura Hispanoamericana,* no. 23 (1998): 713–30.

Hart, Stephen. *César Vallejo: A Literary Biography.* London: Tamesis, 2013.

———. "A Chronology of Vallejo's Life and Works." In Eshleman 2007, 689–704.

———. "Was César Vallejo Guilty as Charged?" *Latin American Literary Review* 26, no. 51 (1998): 79–89.

Higgins, James. "Visión panorámica de la poesía de César Vallejo." In Flores Heredia 2014, 1:223–39.

Martos, Marco, and Elsa Villanueva. *Las palabras de Trilce.* Lima: Seglusa, 1989.

Mattalía, Sonia. "Escalas melografiadas: Vallejo y el vanguardismo narrativo." *Cuadernos Hispanoamericanos. Homenaje a César Vallejo* 1, no. 454–55 (1988): 329–43.

Meo Zilio, Giovanni. *Estudios hispanoamericanos: Temas lingüísticos y de crítica semántica.* Rome: Bulzoni, 1993.

Neale-Silva, Eduardo. *César Vallejo, cuentista: Escrutinio de un múltiple intento de innovación.* Barcelona: Salvat, 1987.

———. *César Vallejo en su face trílcica.* Madison: University of Wisconsin Press, 1975.

———. "Muro este, de César Vallejo." *Thesaurus,* no. 26 (1971): 534–50.

Oviedo y Pérez de Tudela, Rocío. "Vallejo en el umbral de la vanguardia." *Anales de Literatura Hispanoamericana* 2, no. 26 (1997): 363–79.

Patrón Candela, Germán. *El proceso Vallejo*. Trujillo: Universidad Nacional de Trujillo, 1992.

Real Academia Española. *Diccionario de la lengua española*. Barcelona: Espasa Libros, 2014.

Rolland, Romain, Luis Aragon, André Gide, and Paul Vaillant-Couturier, eds. *Commune: Revue littéraire pour la défense de la culture*. Paris: Association des Écrivains et des Artistes Révolutionnaires, 1938.

Susti, Alejandro. "Entre las paredes de la celda: Una revaloración de *Escalas* de César Vallejo." *Revista de crítica literaria latinoamericana* 39, no. 78 (2013): 341–62.

Tárvara Córdova, Francisco. "La justicia en *Escalas*, de César Vallejo." In Flores Heredia 2014, 1:323–43.

Zavaleta, Carlos Eduardo. "Apuntes sobre su prosa: Vallejo en la narrativa peruana actual." *Expreso*, January 3, 2005.

INDEX

Abril de Vivero, Pablo, 125, 154n16. *See also* Paris

acquittal, 123, 144, 146–47. *See also* Godoy, Carlos

Against Professional Secrets, x, xiv, xix

agony, 18, 29

alienation, xiii, xvi

animals: domesticated, 42; horses as, 18, 40, 137, 139; pureness of, 8; spiders as, 5; transitioning species, 55. *See also* beasts; horses; spiders

arson, 23, 145, 151. *See also* acquittal; Santa María, Carlos; Santiago de Chuco; slander

barflies, 10, 34

Baudelaire, Charles, xix, 154n19

beards, xviii, 5, 13, 25, 42

beasts, 5, 139. *See also* animals; horses; spiders

benches, 18–20, 139. *See also* Santiago de Chuco; the sierra

Black Heralds, The, x, 145, 151–52, 153n5

blood: bath, 56; in the body, 9, 37, 41, 43, 45–46, 58, 135; on the body, 20, 22, 40; color of, 35; line, 38, 42, 143

bohemians, 46–47. *See also* Grupo Norte

bread, 19; stale, 12, 28; sweet, 17, 158n33. *See also* breakfast; dinner; lunch; meals

breakfast, xvi, 12, 32. *See also* bread; dinner; lunch; meals

breath: absence of, 43; diabolical, 41; fresh, 52, 58; gasping for, 7; sweet, 150

casinos, 52, 57–58. *See also* gamblers; luck; money

cell block, 124, 127–29, 132; confinement in, xvi, 5, 150; the prisoner

cheekbones, 53, 57

child, the, 36, 58–59, 133, 159n10, 159n11; groan of, 21; narrator, 137; voice of, xvi. *See also* family; father; mother; sisters

circumstance, human, ix, xviii–xix

clocks, 7, 28, 34, 53, 136

Couffon, Claude, xxi–xxii, 155n3

court, criminal, xii, 144–45, 148, 151

crime(s): xvi–xvii, 6, 124, 144–45, 151–52; and criminals, xvii, 6, 10, 23–24; Vallejo charged with, 142

crisis, xi, xv, 48

crowds, 52–53, 56, 58

death, 7–9, 21, 25, 35, 41; as better than life, 24; of brother, xi; of father, xxi; of God, xvii; life and, xviii, 29, 45, 59; of mother, x, 17–18; personification of, 135; in Santiago de Chuco, 123; of Vallejo, xxii

desire, 7, 18, 55, 147

dice, 51–59. *See also* casinos; gamblers; money

dinner, 32–33. *See also* lunch, meals; the table

Dostoevsky, Fyodor, xiv, xix, 154n36

dreams, 7, 17, 28–29, 35, 136, 145

elbows, 10, 37, 51, 53, 150

enigmas, xv, 30, 56, 59. *See also* mystery

family, 24; house of the, 12; Luis Urquizo's, 38–40, 42–43; large,

CÉSAR VALLEJO (1892–1938) was born in the Peruvian Andes and, after publishing some of the most radical Latin American poetry of the twentieth century, moved to Europe, where he diversified his writing practice to encompass theater, fiction, and reportage. As an outspoken alternative to the European avant-garde, Vallejo stands as one of the most authentic and multifaceted creators to write in the Castilian language.

JOSEPH MULLIGAN is a translator and scholar whose work has focused primarily on twentieth-century Latin American *vanguardismo*. He is the translator of *Against Professional Secrets* by César Vallejo (2001) and Gustavo Faverón's novel *The Antiquarian* (2014). Mulligan's translations of Jorge Eduardo Eielson's poems appeared in *Asymmetries: Anthology of Peruvian Poetry* (2015). His translations of Sahrawi poetry appeared in *Poems for the Millennium, vol. 4: The University of California Book of North African Poetry* (2013). He is editor and principal translator of *Selected Writings of César Vallejo* (2015).